The world of vampires and werewolves is in upheaval. The magical community is under attack by a great evil force set to destroy them all and Aaron, their strongest fighter, is oblivious to all around him, his nose glued to his spell book. Yani has given up hope in getting Aaron back on track. He knows he instead has to focus on his own future and the lives of those he loves, even if it means losing Aaron, the love of his life, forever.

But, Yani's life isn't the only one in flux. As the battle heats up and lines are drawn, the rest of his friends must fight for their own survival in a world with no answers to the terrible magic attacking them.

I0584000

JUSTIFIED

Magnified, Book Two

Mell Eight

A NineStar Press Publication

www.ninestarpress.com

Justified

Printed in the USA

ISBN: 978-1-64890-273-4

First Edition, May, 2021

Also available in eBook, ISBN: 978-1-64890-272-7

CONTENT WARNING:
Scenes of graphic supernatural violence and character death.

Prologue

The library was one of the largest rooms inside the Supernatural Coalition of the Northeast's headquarters. The mansion itself was enormous, sprawling across acres of land with dozens of above- and below-ground bedrooms, lounges, and more. The library took up what Yani thought was an entire floor. The librarian was a lamia, and thanks to her extra senses, she could keep track of which book went where. Yani was clueless, since the library didn't use the Dewey Decimal System or have any sort of searchable catalogue.

He chose an aisle and walked slowly along the stacks, reading any titles that happened to catch his attention. Nothing really jumped out at him, so he stopped at a random shelf and read all the titles on it. *We Survived* looked less boring than anything else on the shelf. Yani pulled the book down and headed back to the sitting area closest to the main door.

"I found one," he said triumphantly to Aaron, but Aaron had his head buried in his own book and didn't answer. Yani sighed and turned away to sit on an overstuffed armchair situated nearby. He didn't bother trying to engage Aaron in conversation again. It wouldn't work—at least, not anymore.

Yani opened the book and started reading, hoping it would help pass the time and distract him from the difficulties in his life. It was a short book, only a hundred pages with fairly large print. It wouldn't take too long to read, hopefully just long enough to fill the time before the hearing.

*

Esther wasn't really a special girl. She wasn't overly intelligent or particularly strong. However, she was beautiful, and she understood that her beauty could be used to compensate for what she otherwise lacked. Luckily, Esther wasn't vain. She had been orphaned as a young girl and brought up by her cousin Mordechai, who had kept her grounded in the Jewish faith. Still, he knew how important a chess piece Esther's beauty could be.

"All the beautiful maidens across the land of Persia are required, by dictate of King Ahasuerus, to come to the palace!" The town crier was insistent, repeating the latest dictate for the entire marketplace to hear. Persia was a vast land full of beautiful people, but King Ahasuerus demanded only the best for himself. He needed a wife, Mordechai knew. His last wife had been banished during the full week of drunkenness at the king's recent party. Mordechai didn't know the entire story, only the rumors that circulated the marketplace, but he had seen the now exiled Queen Vashti once before, and only Esther compared to her beauty. King Ahasuerus wouldn't accept anything less.

Queen Vashti, the rumors said, had been asked by the drunken king and courtiers to attend to them wearing only her crown. Garments were not allowed. Vashti had refused, and in a drunken rage, the king had stripped her of her rank and exiled her from Persia. Now sober, King Ahasuerus was apparently having second thoughts.

The crier started to repeat his call, so Mordechai hurried from the market, heading back to his house in the Jewish sector of the city. He had to take a circumventing route. He was Jewish and well known as a leader of the Jewish community. People like him were not welcome in the more affluent areas of Shushan, the capital of Persia that Mordechai called home.

Esther was waiting for him outside the house she shared with Mordechai and his wife and three children. Teres, the man who had run to Mordechai to tell him about the crier's announcement, was standing at her side.

"We have much to speak about," Mordechai told them both. He led the way into the house as he spoke. Esther and Teres followed quickly. Teres sat with Mordechai at the table in the kitchen while Esther made tea.

"The king will want a bride as beautiful as Vashti was," Mordechai insisted. "Women across the land will be traveling to see that they are made the new queen, but, Esther, I think you have the greatest chance."

Esther blushed and shook her head even as she pulled teacups out of the cabinets.

"Mordechai, I doubt he'll choose me. I can hardly be the most beautiful woman in all of Persia, and besides, King Ahasuerus won't choose a Jew for his wife."

"He doesn't have to know you're Jewish," Mordechai replied immediately. "Jews have held their religious ceremonies in secret before. You can certainly do that again in the palace as the new queen."

"You are definitely beautiful enough," Teres added as she leaned over to pour his tea. Mordechai frowned at Teres and made a mental note not to invite Teres over again while Esther was nearby. Teres was a good, learned man. He worked hard for his family and still found time to study the holy texts in the evenings, but he was not the right man for Esther. Mordechai had honestly started to despair ever finding a man who would love Esther for more than her pretty face, but perhaps her pretty face could land her the position of queen. That was worth more to Mordechai and Esther than just finding her a good man to marry.

And so it was settled. Esther left her cousin's home and moved to the palace, where hundreds of beautiful women from around Persia and even beyond were slowly starting to gather. Esther found that she did not enjoy the experience. Women were petty and often cruel.

One by one, the women were paraded across the throne room for King Ahasuerus and his advisers to judge. Esther was in the middle of the very long line of women, and it was days before her turn arrived. She had seen what some of the women had done to others in order to enhance their own chances. Acid in the mercury drops that blinded them horribly, poison in the rouge that had some swooning helplessly and therefore unable to attend their time in front of the king. These were only a few of the horrors Esther had encountered, and she wanted to avoid them all.

On her day to see the king, she refused the fancy makeup and chose a simple robe. The other women who shared the day were covering themselves in makeup, jewels, and fancy silks in order to enhance their beauty. Esther did think about joining them, but when one woman was bitten by a snake hidden in her wardrobe, Esther decided it was better to simply leave the dressing room and join the guards who were waiting to escort the women to the king.

It wasn't too much longer before all the women were ready. They were led to a lavish waiting room, and one by one their names were called. Esther was sixth in line, and as her name was called, she stood and walked behind the guard as they left the room. Whispers followed her about her terrible fashion choices, but she ignored them. King Ahasuerus would see Esther how she was without all the extra frippery, and if he liked her, so be it. Esther would much prefer to be back in Mordechai's house, and perhaps that was the real reason she eschewed the fancier options available to her.

Esther walked slowly across the throne room. She stopped in front of King Ahasuerus, curtsied gracefully, and turned to leave. A gasp rang through the room, and she turned back to see King Ahasuerus's scepter held out to her in invitation. She reached out to touch the tip of the scepter, showing her acceptance of the king's choice.

They would be married with all fanfare within the week.

*

Yani shut the book with a disgusted sigh. He'd thought it might help him pass the afternoon. Now Yani desperately wished he had chosen a completely different stack of books to find a diversion in. The book was so terribly written, the writing style changing perspectives without care for the reader and the prose unbelievably jumpy. It was basically bad fanfiction, if he was totally honest.

The Book of Esther dated back to the earliest days of Jewish exile from the holy land of Jerusalem. No one knew exactly when it had been written or by whom, but it was ten times better than the fanfiction Yani had just been reading based on it.

He set the book aside on one of the reading tables conveniently set up in the sitting area. He looked to the chair next to him and let out another sigh. Aaron hadn't even noticed Yani's disgust. He was probably the only other person in the Supernatural Coalition's compound who could understand why Yani was so unhappy with what he had just read. *The Book of Esther* wasn't a sacred one like the Torah, but the holiday of Purim was important enough to the Jewish people that it had its own traditions and celebrations to go along with it. Jews made triangle-shaped cookies with fruit fillings inside called Hamentashen, which emulated the triangle-shaped hat of the villain in the story, Haman. They partied and drank— it was actually one of the greatest drinking holidays of the Jews—and came together in synagogues to read the *Book of Esther* and celebrate the fact that Haman's plan to exterminate all the Jews of Persia had been foiled thanks to Esther's hard work.

Aaron wasn't reading to pass the time, however. Yani knew that, so he shouldn't begrudge his boyfriend of two years for ignoring his huffing. Aaron was studying Kabbalah.

As a mage of some power, Aaron could hold his own against just about every supernatural creature they encountered. Combined with Yani's ability to see through illusions, Luke's ability to traverse the dreams of those around him, and Brandon's strength as a werewolf, Aaron led the most formidable team the Supernatural Coalition had. Aaron's magic wasn't ordinary, though. Both of his parents were witches and had taught him the basic magic most witches used today, but his mother came from a line of Kabbalists and had been teaching Aaron everything she knew. His current homework was to read the Zohar, a medieval book on Kabbalism. It had been written after Kabbalah had been taken over by learned Jewish men who couldn't use the magic in the first and second centuries, but wanted the wisdom inherent in Kabbalah.

Today's cadre of Kabbalism would never accept Aaron's mother, but her magic and her son's were cleverly hidden within those ancient texts. Aaron wanted to know what the men who studied those texts today had written, so he was reading the Zohar.

Apparently, the Zohar was very interesting. Aaron was completely engrossed, turning the pages slowly as he read and murmuring things under his breath. Yani didn't know if there were magical spells in there, although he doubted it. Modern Judaic Kabbalism, meaning from medieval times to the present, declared any magical connotations within the literature to be anathema. Aaron might actually have more luck reading the books on Cabala, the modern, non-Jewish interpretation of the study. Nothing was anathema in Cabala, magic included, although it tended to draw in Hollywood stars more than actual theorists or believers. Most of what Yani knew about it he had learned secondhand through Aaron anyway. Yani couldn't use magic, but he worked every day with Aaron and lived with him, even when they weren't working, and had been picking up the lingo.

Yani was glad Aaron's book was interesting at least, since the Purim fanfiction Yani had found was so abysmal.

He rolled his eyes as he picked up the book again. He really had nothing else to do, and the Coalition's library was so large he doubted he would be able to quickly find anything better. Yani flipped to the end of the story, hoping the climax in the *Book of Esther* wouldn't be too butchered. If he finished reading it before Aaron was done studying for the day, Yani would brave the stacks to see if he could find something else to read.

For the moment, he let himself get pulled back into the book with a grimace of distaste.

*

"You must, Esther!" Mordechai insisted. He held his hands out imploringly, which only emphasized the fact that he was wearing the ripped sackcloth of a man in mourning. Haman had set a date, and the gallows were being built even as Mordechai pleaded with Esther.

"If I dare approach King Ahasuerus without him asking for me first, he'll have my head removed!" Esther gasped. Mordechai knew she wasn't lying, but the situation warranted it.

"Let me tell you a story that will make it clearer," Mordechai finally replied. He had snuck into the palace to see her under the cover of darkness, when all of her ladies-in-waiting would be dismissed for the night. No one would bother them for hours, so Mordechai settled deeper into his chair and waited for Esther to finish pacing and take the chair across from him.

"You know the story of Joseph, how his brothers cruelly sold him into slavery in Egypt and he was eventually able to save all of Egypt from a terrible famine? Well, generations later, Egypt still thrived and the Jewish descendants of Joseph and his family had their own village. One day Pharaoh, who had forgotten what Joseph had done for Egypt, looked out across his land and saw the Israelite village. He knew the Israelites were different than the Egyptians. They prayed to one god instead of many, they dressed differently, they ate differently, and their customs and culture were different from the rest of Egypt. They were not Egyptian to Pharaoh in the least bit. Pharaoh turned to his advisers and asked: 'Should we be invaded, what guarantee do I have that those Israelites will not side with my enemy in war?' His advisers could not give him an answer. So Pharaoh enslaved the Israelites and declared that all sons born to them should be killed at birth. He wanted to decimate their population and make it impossible for the Israelites to form an army against him at his very doorstep.

"His is the first recorded declaration that the death of the Jews was preferable to any other form of discrimination, and Haman looks to continue Pharaoh's failed quest. You can stop him, Esther, just as Moses was able to stop Pharaoh. Can you be our Moses in our time of need?" Mordechai was begging, but he felt no embarrassment over it. He had to save his people, and Esther was their only chance.

So Esther agreed. She fasted for three days in preparation, then approached the king. Ahasuerus lowered his scepter to her, so she didn't die that day. She threw a great party and then explained to her husband that she would die in the morning, hanged from the gallows Haman had so gallantly built. The next morning, instead of sending Esther and Mordechai to the noose, King Ahasuerus hanged Haman. A day of celebration was declared, and Jews throughout Persia and all across the world still rejoice to this day.

The End.

*

Yani snorted with disgust and snapped the book shut yet again. In addition to the terrible writing, the author had taken extreme liberties with the actual plot. The entire climax of the original story had been reduced to a few quick lines on a page. The author had also randomly thrown in the story of Moses for good measure.

And yet, the author did bring up a rather poignant message. African Americans were kidnapped from their homes, shipped overseas, and turned into slaves. Native Americans were marched from their homes to a new, less desirable location. Roma were shunned and forced to live nomadic lives. There were dozens of similar stories scattered throughout history of singular groups suffering because they were different. Many of those stories ended in death, but there was only one story that guaranteed death for the unfortunate victim every time. Pharaoh had called for the death of the Jews, Haman had called for the death of the Jews, and Hitler had forcibly gathered up the Jews and brutally murdered them.

Iran had promised that their first nuclear weapon would be fired at Israel. Hamas's charter called for the extermination of every Jew. It was a familiar trope repeated throughout history that Yani was more than passably aware of. He had grown up with the story, and apparently so had the author of the terrible Purim fanfiction. Plus, Yani had taken classes on genocides and human rights dilemmas and had noticed there weren't any other instances where one people was purposefully and repeatedly rounded up and sentenced to death simply because they were different from the norm.

He really was failing miserably at distracting himself.

Yani groaned under his breath and slumped in his chair. He had tried reading a book, but that hadn't worked, and then he had even allowed himself to try thinking deep and meaningful thoughts. That had been unsuccessful too. He couldn't stop his gaze from drifting across the room to where Aaron was obliviously reading his oh-so-important text. Yani wanted to speak with him, to say hello, or at the very least get some acknowledgement that Yani was nearby. He hadn't gotten a single thing, and it was starting to drive him mad.

How long had it been since they had shared more than a brief kiss good morning? If Yani couldn't even remember that, he definitely didn't want to try calculating how long it had been since they'd had sex. They had chosen to live their lives together, but every day it felt like they were drifting further and further apart.

It didn't make any sense to Yani. His heart was absolutely still set on Aaron—there was no denying that absolute truth—yet his brain couldn't help pointing out all the little things that said their relationship just wasn't working anymore. The lack of sex or even any romantic moments, the fact that Aaron was across the room and hadn't even noticed Yani sitting nearby, and a dozen other little things had all combined to sow doubts in Yani's brain.

Their schism was justified, though. At least, that was what Aaron had said the one time Yani had tried to confront him about it. They needed to defeat Cain, the strange and powerful enemy who had managed to subdue them all effortlessly two years ago. They had only escaped in one piece thanks to a bit of luck, and ever since then, everyone had immersed themselves in their studies to try to become more powerful. They needed to be much stronger to even have a chance against Cain.

Yani had learned everything he could about his special vision. He had an ability called eyes-that-see, which basically meant illusions and glamours had no effect on him. His powers had been increased dramatically thanks to Cain, who had drawn a spell in fresh blood on Yani's skin to enhance Yani's eyes with the intent to then steal those powers and kill Yani. Since then, Yani had tested his eyes on every kind of illusion or glamour he could find, trying to learn how to distinguish what type of spells he was encountering and how to properly describe what he was seeing to Aaron, Luke, and Brandon, who were then tasked with finding a way to dispel the illusion. Yani could also see spells and had been working hard to learn how to read them so Aaron didn't have to waste precious energy working his own spell to allow him to see what Yani could in order to then decipher it.

Brandon was Yani's college roommate and close friend. He had been working on becoming a better werewolf. He was from a line of alphas, but the ability to control that inherent power only came from great discipline. He had to master his wolf side and fully integrate it with his human side to completely embrace the strength of being a werewolf. Brandon had dozens of siblings and cousins who should have been above him in the pecking order of the werewolf pack, but he was quickly rising to the top.

Luke, Brandon's boyfriend, had taken Cain's attack very personally. Cain had forced Luke into the realm of dreams and kept him there against his will. As an incubus, a creature whose power over dreams and lust was supposed to be unparalleled, that was the utmost insult. Yani didn't really understand what Luke had to do to get stronger, although it had to have something to do with sex, but he was doing it. He could throw someone in and out of the dream plane effortlessly without the need of a door. He could also force someone into sleep by pulling their mind to the dream plane. It was a great way to interrogate people, but it was also perfect for subduing an attacker. If they were asleep, they couldn't stop themselves from being captured.

Brandon and Luke were a couple. They had been together for a few months longer than Yani and Aaron, but their relationship hadn't faltered. Despite their need to train and practice, Brandon and Luke still managed to maintain a happy and lasting partnership. Yani couldn't understand what was going wrong between him and Aaron. Their need to grow stronger shouldn't come between them, but somehow it had, and Yani couldn't figure out how to fix it.

"We're ready for you now," Orath's voice, his Scandinavian accent a heavy lilt, called from the door. Yani looked up at him, grateful for the distraction.

"Is it that time already?" Aaron murmured. He placed his bookmark into the book and closed it gently before standing to join Orath at the door. Yani stood too, and Aaron turned toward him in surprise. "When did you get here?" he asked, but Yani could tell his mind wasn't entirely on the question. His eyes had the slightly unfocused look he got whenever he was working on a new spell.

Yani had only said hello to Aaron three times before deciding to go find a book instead. He stomped past Aaron without answering. He knew where the meeting room was located, so he nodded to Orath and kept walking down the hall. Aaron would catch up on his own.

The coalition's mansion was hidden away in a thick forest just north of Boston. Other supernatural creatures had their own houses in and around the nearby town, including the werewolf and vampire houses adjacent to the coalition building, but the mansion itself had been built to house any and all magical creatures needing a place to stay. The ceilings were tall and the halls Yani walked through were wide to accommodate those with height and/or girth. There weren't any windows, so nocturnal creatures could wander during the day should they choose to, and the overhead lighting wasn't too bright, to protect delicate vision. Everything was beautifully decorated, though. The walls were a gentle shade of cream, the floors dark hardwood, and the lighting tasteful. Yani couldn't complain about anything to be perfectly honest.

Except for the fact that Aaron was walking behind Yani and Orath with his nose stuck in that damned book again.

Yani knew firsthand how important it was to get stronger. He had scars and nightmares, the same as Aaron. There was no excuse for what Aaron was doing. None.

The room that had been set aside as a hearing room used to be an old dining room. The space was meant to hold over a hundred people in comfort. The long tables and chairs had been removed two years ago when Bishop, the alpha of the Charles River Pack and president of the Supernatural Coalition of the Northeast, had come up with the idea of sending teams like Yani's. Claims of violence, territory theft, and other issues used to be handled between the two communities in conflict, but that normally ended up in more violence. Bishop wanted to quell the fighting in order to save lives and to help keep the existence of supernatural creatures secret from the rest of the world. Yani's team traveled to find facts and bring that information back to a hearing session.

Which was what Yani was walking into at the moment. A raised dais had been erected in the front of the room. Bishop sat behind a desk there. His white hair and wrinkled face looked very dignified in the hushed room as Yani and Aaron walked inside. Aaron's book had vanished sometime between the hallway and the door.

There were two long tables set up just below the dais, one on each side of Bishop's desk, where the two claimants sat. Behind those was another long table, centered in-between the other two. Yani headed to the empty table and took a chair. Aaron took the chair next to him, and a few seconds later, Luke and Brandon hurried in and took their own seats. Next in line were chairs for any interested people to sit and watch the proceedings. Orath took a spot at the side of the room, and one glance at him kept everyone calmly in their seats during the proceedings. Orath was one of the creatures that needed the high ceilings, and no one wanted to tangle with him.

"We are ready to begin," Bishop called. "The case was brought forward by Arden Ofkerent, a miller from southern Maine, and his daughter, Desire Ofkerent." Both were sitting at the table in front of Yani and slightly to his left. The miller was balding, but he was only in his forties, and his arms and back were strong from the difficult work he did every day. "They accuse Martlestiltskin, a leprechaun, living just over the state border in New Hampshire, of attempting to trick Desire out of her firstborn child two years ago."

That put Desire at only sixteen years old, well under the acceptable age limit established by modern supernatural coalitions across the first world. Desire was a pretty girl with long, gently curling blonde hair and big blue eyes. She was also six months pregnant—although Yani did notice that the father of her child was not at the proceedings—and had told her father about what Martlestiltskin had done when the pregnancy test had come back positive. Arden had immediately contacted Bishop's representative in order to have the promise made between Desire and Martlestiltskin invalidated and to demand restitution.

Martlestiltskin was a small man, barely five feet tall. He didn't have the orange hair or beard prevalent in cartoons, but his skin did have an odd tint of green. Leprechauns gained power through granting wishes. They made a trade, a bit of fluff in return for something greater, and with each exchange a leprechaun grew. His five feet was tall for a leprechaun, but then, he had been preying on children.

"Martlestiltskin, do you have anything to add to the proceedings?" Bishop asked now that he had outlined the case.

Martlestiltskin shrugged. "Never trust a miller or his daughter," he spat. "Should've listened to the old stories, I should."

"Arden, do you have anything to add?" Bishop turned to Arden and Desire when it became clear that Martlestiltskin wouldn't be saying anything more.

"No, sir," Arden replied immediately with a firm nod to Bishop. "He went after my daughter when she was still a child. I... We want our restitution for his crimes."

Bishop turned to the center table where Yani, Aaron, Brandon, and Luke were sitting. "The coalition's investigative team will now outline their findings."

Aaron stood up. "We traveled to each of their homes," he explained. "The area surrounding the leprechaun's home was very troubled. A six-year-old girl wanted a pony for her birthday, which her parents rightfully ignored, yet a brown-and-white pony was found eating their front lawn the morning the girl turned seven. Three gold necklaces went missing that same day. A fifteen-year-old boy broke his arm two days before he was supposed to pitch in the championship baseball game for his junior varsity team. On the day of the game he was miraculously healed, but the trophy his team won was stolen. In total, we have documented three dozen such incidents, all involving underage children."

Bishop nodded thoughtfully. "Thank you, Aaron. It is clear, Martlestiltskin, that you have formed a habit of preying on children. No other leprechauns were found in the area, I presume?" he added to Aaron.

"None that we could locate," Aaron replied. "The next closest one is in northern Maine, hidden somewhere deep in the marshlands."

"Then the verdict is clear. Martlestiltskin, under the authority of this coalition, you are hereby stripped of all powers and magics you gained from preying on innocent children. You are required to return every single trinket taken and promise made." As Bishop spoke, Martlestiltskin began to shrink in size. He was down to three feet tall by the time Bishop finished and glaring hatefully at Arden and Desire.

"What about our restitution?" Arden asked.

"Ah, yes. That is the next part of our agenda," Bishop said with a nod. "Aaron?"

"Once we had finished gathering our findings on Martlestiltskin, we traveled to the Ofkerents' hometown." Arden started looking pale as Aaron spoke, Yani saw with an inward touch of glee. "There we found the birth certificate of one Desire A. Ofkerent, age twenty-five. Two years ago, when she allegedly made her promise with Martlestiltskin, she was already twenty-three. Eighteen is the age of consent. In addition, we spoke with a local seamstress working to take in Ms. Ofkerent's party dress for a celebration she's attending next week at a nearby hotel. She was shocked to hear Ms. Ofkerent was pregnant as Desire had only been in to see her a month ago and she had lost weight."

They had told Bishop all of this before the hearing, but he was still frowning as Aaron finished outlining their findings.

"It is clear there are two cases here. The first, Martlestiltskin preying on children, has been properly dealt with. The second is the Ofkerents' attempt to take advantage of the coalition and Martlestiltskin's bad behavior for monetary gain.

"Desire Ofkerent, your firstborn child belongs to Martlestiltskin as you promised. This hearing cannot and will not change what you, a consenting adult, agreed upon. The Supernatural Coalition of the Northeast will ensure you follow up on your promise. In addition, you attempted to coerce one hundred thousand dollars in restitution out of Martlestiltskin and this coalition. You owe fifty thousand to the coalition and fifty thousand to Martlestiltskin in restitution for the time and pain you put both through in your scheme. A payment schedule will be arranged for you."

"Why should we give any money to that creature?" Arden snarled, his face bright red.

"Think of it as an investment for your grandchild, since he'll be taking care of them," Bishop replied with a growl. "This case is closed. Orath, please see that Mr. and Ms. Ofkerent are escorted from the premises. Martlestiltskin and I will leave from a different door." He stood and gestured for Martlestiltskin to follow him out a side entrance while Orath stood menacingly over the Ofkerents until they were herded out the main doors.

Yani waited with Aaron, Luke, and Brandon until they were certain the hallway was clear, then followed Luke and Brandon out of the room. Aaron would no doubt go back to his damned book, and Yani much preferred to have dinner with people who would actually talk to him.

*

Maki knew there was something wrong the moment she stepped out of her small cabin and into the woods. Something didn't quite smell right. All the usual scents of pine and rotting leaves were present as they were supposed to be, but there was something deeper to that rotting smell that wasn't sitting well with her. It wasn't the scent of an animal carcass left behind, nor did she smell any blood. Still, a shiver of fear crawled up her spine.

That wouldn't do, Maki firmly reminded herself. She wasn't allowed to be scared. Okasan had been very firm about that. Maki's mother had spent far too much of her childhood afraid, and she hadn't wanted Maki to have the same terrible experiences. It was why the entire family had moved from California to the East Coast after the end of World War II, despite being the only werepandas in the region. They were far more prevalent in the western half of the United States, as that was where many Chinese immigrants had settled. Japanese werepandas were rare, but they did exist, and Maki's family was from a long line of proud pandas.

None of which explained what was wrong in the woods.

She didn't live in an isolated house on purpose, but she couldn't see her neighbors' houses through the thick foliage. Given how high in the Adirondack Mountains her house was, that wasn't unusual. She had chosen the area because there were a lot of werebears living in the vicinity, and it was nice to spend time with her own kind, even though they didn't form packs like wolves. Maki knew she ought to go back into her house and call someone about the odd smell. Arnold, the general leader of all the bears who made the mountain range their home, was a kind man. He was also a busy man. Maki didn't want to bother him for something that might mean she was coming down with a summer cold and her sense of smell was slightly off.

Maki hopped down from the porch and walked across the short span of cut grass in front of her house and entered the woods. The area was rocky and required no small amount of climbing ability to traverse. The paved streets had been carved from the mountain itself, as had the flattened land her small house sat on. Everywhere else was hill and cliff. It was a perfect place for a bear to climb and wander without worry that a human would get in the way. She did like living up here, although sometimes she wished there was someone to share her home with. Finding someone who understood her peculiarities as a were was difficult enough, but finding someone who respected the fact that she was a panda in a land of black and brown bears had proven to be impossible.

She shook that depressing thought from her head and refocused on following the rotten smell. Luckily, it didn't take too long to locate. Her favorite television show was going to be on in twenty minutes, and she didn't want to miss it.

It looked like a hawk had killed a squirrel. There was a wide, bloody slash mark down the side of the squirrel, something a set of talons could do. The hawk had been scared away, possibly by her arrival, before it could begin feasting.

That didn't explain the rotten smell in the air. The kill looked fresh, the blood red on the ground. Flies hadn't even started feeding off the carcass yet. Maki took one step closer, leaning over the squirrel to sniff.

Looking down at the bloody remains was the last thing she remembered before her vision went red and her head went blank.

*

Blood was dripping from her paws, Maki realized. She blinked and her vision slowly refocused. Maki had no idea why everything was so blurry, but she had to shut her eyes for a long moment and reopen them twice before she could visually confirm what she could feel. Blood covered her body, and bits of fur and skin were caught in her claws. She was in her panda form, yet she had no memory of transforming her shape.

Maki didn't feel injured, so she didn't think any of the blood was hers. The fur on her paws was also brown, a color she didn't have in her pelt.

So where had it all come from?

"There she is!"

The shout was full of anger and fear. Growling answered as many large figures crashed through the thick trees. Werebears in human and bear form circled her in moments. Maki held up her paws, knowing that the dripping blood wouldn't placate anyone.

"You've killed them all," one of the weres in human form snarled.

Maki opened her mouth to ask what he was talking about, but in her panda form, she couldn't speak. Who had she killed? She had absolutely no idea what they were talking about.

Arnold stepped closer. He was in human form and had what appeared to be three long slashes bleeding across his chest. They looked like someone had raked claws down his chest. Maki glanced at her own bloody claws and couldn't help wondering if maybe some of Arnold's blood was mixed in.

But she hadn't called Arnold before leaving her house. Maki remembered having that mental conversation with herself and deciding not to bother him.

Why had she left her house again? There was a reason, but she couldn't remember it.

"Calm down, Maki," Arnold said once it was clear he had her attention. "Shift back into human form, and we can talk about this."

"Talk about it?" the first were snarled. "We're going to execute her for what she's done."

Execute! What the hell had happened? She looked around, but still didn't see any clues.

"Shift back, Maki. We need to talk first, see what the problem is," Arnold insisted.

Maki nodded. Hopefully, Arnold would be able to explain what had happened, because Maki certainly didn't know. She tried to call on her body to shift forms, focusing on having human arms and legs again. Nothing happened. She tried a second time, straining to let the magic flow through her body. Nothing.

She turned panicked eyes on Arnold, hoping he would understand despite the fact that she couldn't talk. He frowned at her. Maki tried a third time, but there was no spark of magic. It was like she had lost her human form entirely.

"Okay, Maki. Okay," Arnold said, holding out his hands toward her when she whimpered.

"Not okay!" the first bear cut in. "I say we kill her now. Why wait?"

"Because we're civilized people," Arnold replied immediately. "We'll bring her to the coalition. They'll have people able to force her back into human form. She'll be made to talk, to explain what she did, and then they'll decide on an appropriate punishment."

"We're going to let some mangy wolves decide how our sleuth runs itself?"

Maki didn't know the bear who wanted her dead, but she did try to remain on the outskirts of their society. As a bear, she was welcome among them, but because she was a panda, she was still ostracized. So far, Maki had only met Arnold and a few select others.

"We are going to let a court of law handle the issue. We're not animals," Arnold insisted. His power as their leader flared, filling the space around them with oppressive strength. "We are rational, thinking beings, and it is with that mindset that we are going to move forward." The other bears shrank back under Arnold's onslaught. The one arguing snorted to convey his disgust. "Maki, come down the mountain with me. We have to cage you for travel since you can't transform. You understand?"

Maki nodded to show she understood. She still had no idea what she had done, but surely someone in the coalition could help her figure it out.

The coalition was her only chance to avoid execution for something she had no memory of committing.

*

Yani was just pulling back the covers on the bed when someone knocked on the front door. He straightened his boxers to double-check that he was decent before going to answer it. Aaron was sitting on the couch next to the door, still in his slacks and button-up shirt from the hearing earlier that day, with his head buried in that damned book again. Yani had doubts he would even come to bed.

Brandon was standing outside the door when Yani unlocked and opened it. He waved away Yani's gesture to come inside.

"Just wanted to let you know we've another case," Brandon explained. It was eleven o'clock at night, but that didn't stop Brandon's grandfather, Bishop Karr, from calling his grandson whenever he wanted. Brandon had always been muscular, but his thin and lanky frame had hid it. Over the past few years, since they'd both graduated from college, he had started putting on more muscle mass. His shoulders were broader and his arms thicker, but that only added to his rakish good looks. Brandon's dirty-blond hair was still unkempt and a little long on the collar, and his sparkling eyes always said he was ready for the next bit of fun.

Brandon's gaze drifted toward Yani's shoulder as they always did whenever Yani was wearing anything without sleeves. He had a puckered, round scar there with blackened edges like a piece of charcoal. It was from an unfortunate encounter with an ifrit djinni. Yani still had nightmares about it, and Brandon couldn't help studying the mark every time he saw it to spot any changes. It didn't hurt, but Yani's eyes-that-see told him it was still burning even all these years later.

"Another one?" Yani asked, trying to divert Brandon's attention. "We just wrapped up the last one. We usually get at least a week's break."

Brandon shrugged. "Gramps just got the phone call. He said the werebears are bringing down a suspect who killed four wild bears in some sort of rampage and then attacked them too when they tried to stop her. They want a proper trial and sentencing, so Gramps says we're up."

"When do they arrive?"

"Tomorrow morning," Brandon explained. "They're coming from the Adirondacks, somewhere called Bolton Landing, and they apparently stuck one of their sleuth that's still in bear form in an animal trailer. It's about a five-hour drive, plus having to cart the trailer through the mountains. Gramps says he'll get them settled in when they arrive, and then we'll speak to both sides. He wants us on the road by Monday."

Yani nodded, but he was only half listening to Brandon. The best way to get to the Adirondack Mountains was to travel through Albany. Yani had been to Lake George plenty of times as a kid. It was a great place to spend a warm summer afternoon swimming in the lake and exploring the old town. Bolton Landing was only one additional exit north on the highway.

"Do you mind if I leave right after we finish talking to both parties?" Yani asked. "It would be nice to spend the weekend with my parents before starting work with you on Monday."

"Just you?" Brandon asked with a glance over Yani's shoulder to where Aaron still had his nose in that damn book.

Yani hesitated for a long moment before answering, hoping that Aaron would lift his head and reply that of course he was going with Yani. That didn't happen. "Just me," he confirmed around the lump forming in his throat.

Brandon nodded, seeming to understand that anything he said would not help. "I assume you'll take a bus down? We can pick you up on Monday when we get to Albany, no problem." He reached out to clasp Yani tightly on the shoulder as if to remind Yani that they were still friends, even if Aaron was being an idiot, before turning and heading back down the stairs.

The house had been converted into two separate apartments, one on the first floor and one on the second. Yani and Aaron had jokingly forced Brandon and Luke to take the first floor, declaring that they refused to be kept awake at night because the ceiling was squeaking rhythmically. Werewolves and incubi couldn't keep it in their pants, and Brandon and Luke were perfect examples. Yani liked the little apartment he shared with Aaron and the fact that his best friends were just downstairs. At least, he had liked it before Aaron had turned into a butt.

Yani closed and locked the door, then headed back to the bedroom and his solitary bed, wondering whether Aaron might actually join him that night.

Yani fell asleep before Aaron appeared, and when he woke in the morning, he was still alone.

Their relationship was clearly failing, and Yani had no idea what to do to fix it. Talking to—or even yelling at—Aaron was pointless, since Aaron didn't even acknowledge Yani was there, and the one time Yani had yanked the book from Aaron's hands, Aaron had placidly taken the book back without even noticing Yani's ire. Nothing he had tried had worked. Yani got up to shower for the day with a sinking heart. It was over. There was no way to salvage the best boyfriend he'd ever had.

Now all he had to do was tear Aaron away from that book for long enough to tell him.

*

Antoinette was beautiful. She was powerful. She was the leader of all the vampires in the entirety of the Northeast. That was something to be lauded, and she had to admit she greatly enjoyed the admiration. Her life up to this point hadn't exactly been good.

In 1823, she was born a slave in the South Caribbean to a mother and father who were owned. As soon as the master and his overseers thought she was old enough, she had been put to work in the tobacco fields alongside her parents. The sun had been hot overhead, the whip merciless on her back, and her days had been full of endless toil with no positive results.

Sold at age seven with four other young slaves, she had never seen her parents again. Her new master was strange in the head. She'd received a nice uniform, good rations, and even a real bed in the basement of his opulent house. The first time he'd put his hand under her skirt to feel her thigh, she'd endured it. There weren't any whips in this house, and at the time, that had meant more to her. When his hand had started drifting upward as Antoinette grew older, she'd hit him.

Undesirable slaves, even those like her who were still technically children, were sent to menial labor designed to kill them after only a few months of working them to the bone. Her master's nose had bled after she'd hit him, so he'd sent her to the docks as undesirable. That had been hard, backbreaking work, and she'd almost regretted her indiscretion, but at the same time, she'd known she couldn't allow anyone to touch her like her master had tried to do. It just wasn't right.

Her chains had slipped free from her wrists one night thanks to how desperately thin she had become. In only half a moment she decided to run. There was nowhere safe to hide on an island, but ships came and went all day. Somehow Antoinette managed to sneak aboard one and remain hidden all the way to England.

There she had scrounged as a street rat, learning the language spoken only by her masters back home. A new master had eventually picked her up when she was twelve. This master was cruel in a new way. He'd wanted her blood and her eternal slavery, locking her away in his underground chambers for the next hundred and fifty years. It had taken her much longer to escape him, and when she'd emerged, it was to a new world.

Cars, telephones, and other such wondrous technology had been invented. Slavery had ended, and she was free for the first time in her life. Yet at the same time, she was forever trapped.

Her last master had changed her into a creature of the night just like him when she was only twelve years old. The new world demanded to know where her parents were, who watched over her, and where she slept at night. She couldn't become a street rat again and risk exposure to sunlight, nor could she remain hidden. The local vampire community had located her almost immediately.

She found it strange to be among the beautiful and privileged. The English vampires were creatures who had known power and prestige for centuries. Antoinette was nothing like them; she felt like a slave standing among her masters. They didn't purposefully belittle her, but it was difficult for her to discover who she was amid their overwhelming presence.

When a group of vampires arranged to visit America, Antoinette joined them and remained behind when they left again. The American vampires were coarse and crude in comparison to the European ones. They didn't believe in pomp and prestige, instead focusing on actual power. The vampire who had changed her had given her a powerful lineage, but at the same time, her apparent youth gave an illusion that she was powerless.

For the next thirty years, Antoinette existed in a strange role—stuck between the powerful and the helpless. At first, she hadn't noticed when vampires she used to see regularly disappeared; then she'd hidden with the rest of the coven until a master vampire from Europe came to find her.

He called himself Martin, although she had a feeling that name was one he had chosen for modern times. He was ancient, far older than any vampire she had ever met. Somehow Martin had injected power into her body, and she had grown. The twelve-year-old body was gone forever, replaced with one belonging to a strong and supple twenty-year-old. When Martin had to return to his own home and coven in Poland, she became the new master of the Boston coven.

Yet Antoinette didn't know or understand what it meant to be an adult or in charge of others since she had never been trained. The learning curve was far too steep, and the broken coven she was supposed to lead back to strength eventually scattered to other parts of the world. In the end, she led only the very few others who had remained behind.

At night Antoinette roamed the basement halls of the vampire house and the coalition building. She had nothing better to do, and it helped allay her boredom. She met all sorts of strange and interesting creatures hidden away in the dark recesses. However, tonight, the strange, choked crying she heard down one of the better-lit hallways was different.

Antoinette went to investigate, curious to learn something new.

A panda was sobbing, curled into the corner of one of the coalition's few jail cells. Antoinette studied the creature for a few moments, trying to decide what sort of being she was looking at. She finally decided on a werepanda, despite having never heard of their kind before.

"Hysterical crying isn't going to get you out of here," Antoinette said.

The panda jumped in surprise, spinning around and rubbing one big paw beneath her eyes to wipe away tears.

"They're really not bad people, the coalition. You just have to tell them what happened, and they'll do their best to prove your innocence. It's this strange American custom. Took me forever to get used to it."

The panda waved her paws, first at herself and then at the cell around her. Antoinette tilted her head, trying to understand. It wasn't until the panda closed her arms around herself as if she were stuck that Antoinette got it.

"You can't shift back," Antoinette guessed, and the panda nodded. "The coalition has a pretty strong mage who might be able to figure out why you're stuck. Do you know if he visited you?" The panda shrugged. "Strange that he hasn't. I'll ask around, see if I can find out why, and get him down here to try getting you to shift back."

The panda looked so hopeful Antoinette couldn't help smiling at her.

"We'll have you back to rights soon enough, and then you can explain your innocence and get out of here. Don't worry." Someone who cried as if all hope was lost like the panda was doing couldn't be guilty.

Antoinette leaned against the wall across from the bars of the cell and couldn't help grinning when the panda gracefully sank onto the floor where she could look at Antoinette.

"I've never seen a werepanda before," Antoinette said despite knowing the panda couldn't answer. "Although I guess that makes sense. There are so many different types of were-animals out there. Everyone always thinks of werewolves because of the stories, but werepandas don't appear in the pages of a book, howling at the moon."

The panda frowned at Antoinette as if to say, "Of course pandas don't howl at the moon; we're far more civilized than that." Antoinette let out a laugh that she quickly muffled with one hand before the noise attracted any unwanted attention. When Antoinette looked up at her again, the panda was shrugging awkwardly. There was almost a smile on the panda's face, as if seeing Antoinette laugh had helped dispel some of the gloom.

Suddenly, Antoinette wanted nothing more than to make the panda smile again. Antoinette wanted to make the panda laugh, and cry with happiness, but most of all she wanted to know the panda's name. Just who was this intriguing creature locked away in the bowels of the coalition?

Antoinette stayed with the panda for hours, enjoying the one-sided chatting until the pull of the rising sun forced her to leave. She would be back, though, and hopefully with the mage who could fix the panda so their one-sided conversation could instead be a shared one.

Chapter One

Rain

"Seriously, why doesn't Yani have his own car yet?"

The whine was achingly familiar, and Yani couldn't help smiling slightly to himself as he tossed his small suitcase into the trunk and walked around the car to hop in the front passenger seat.

"Because I'm still not suicidal," Yani explained for the hundredth time. Driving in Boston was doable, but he had taken his driving test in the much tamer city of Albany. The Boston cars whipping around the curves on skinny roads that had originally been designed to handle horse-drawn carriages were difficult enough to avoid on foot, let alone while in a car.

"Your friends have a car." Shira sniffed with a toss of her artfully cut bangs. "And you don't actually live in Boston any longer."

Both true. Yani didn't have a snappy comeback for that. "It's a company car," he tried to explain rationally, but he already knew rationality and his thirteen-year-old sister did not coexist in the same general area.

"Yani is only staying with us for a long weekend," Dad interjected before Shira could really get going. "What time are your friends coming?"

"Sometime on Monday. It depends on what time they're able to leave Boston, so three and a half hours later, I'll be heading to Lake George."

"What business does your company have up there?" Dad asked.

Yani's parents had always been a little suspicious of Yani's job. It sounded too much like something that was too good to be true. Being hired right out of college with a good salary and benefits was something that did happen, but to be hired with his boyfriend and two best friends and then to work alongside them? Both Dad and Mom had voiced their reservations to Yani at some point. Plus, Yani had decided the best way to avoid having to explain all the supernatural stuff they wouldn't understand was to say he had to sign a confidentiality clause and couldn't actually tell them what he really did.

Put like that, Yani totally understood why his parents probably thought he worked for the mob. He couldn't tell them he instead worked for a werewolf.

"One of their companies has been having some trouble," Yani tried to explain, wincing when every word only emphasized how illegal it sounded. "We're supposed to figure out what went wrong and help fix it."

Albany wasn't technically in New England, but it didn't have a coalition of its own. There was one in Buffalo, but it only covered Rochester and Syracuse, the cities far to the west of Albany. Another coalition handled everything in New York City, but they only went as far north as Poughkeepsie. The supernatural residents of Albany could choose to contact one of those two coalitions if they wanted to keep an issue in state. However, the Massachusetts border, and therefore the edge of the New England Coalition, was only a few miles to the east of Albany, considerably closer than any other coalition. Many residents of Albany and the surrounding area, Lake George and Bolton Landing included, gave their support to New England, which was why Yani occasionally got called home to Albany for work.

"Boring," Shira grumbled. "Why don't you get a real job with a real car?"

"How are your bat mitzvah lessons going?" Yani asked to change the subject.

Shira huffed. "God, Yani. Get a life!" She crossed her arms in the back seat and turned her head to glare at passing traffic. Conversation closed.

Unfortunately, or maybe it was fortunately, her bat mitzvah was only a few months away. Shira's birthday was in August, only a week and a half from today, but summer bat mitzvahs were always difficult. Friends and family were out of town with plans for the summer and couldn't make it. September had the high holidays taking up most of the available Saturdays, so Shira's bat mitzvah date was in October. It was still a touchy subject for her, and as the dutiful older brother, Yani had to push that button as many times as possible.

This was the distraction he needed. There was nothing quite like the normality of home to keep him grounded in a world where his life was about as abnormal as it could get. He was going to take the time without any worries to figure out how he was going to move on with his life without Aaron in it.

That thought tightened his throat and had him blinking back tears. It took him a moment, but he had himself back under control before Shira noticed.

It wasn't too much longer before they got back home. Shira was on summer break from school and had been dragged along to pick Yani up. Mom must have been home making dinner, since she wasn't with them. Dad drove the car up their driveway and slotted it into the garage next to Mom's car. They all got out, and Yani grabbed his suitcase from the trunk.

Shira was long gone by the time Yani got inside. Mom was sprawled on the couch in front of the TV. The kitchen was dark, but it was Friday; they would be having Shabbat dinner that night eventually.

Mom groaned as she levered herself off the couch. "The steaks are done marinating. Mike, can you start the grill?"

Dad nodded and walked to the back door leading to the deck. Mom turned to Yani next.

"Where's Aaron?" she asked, looking over Yani's shoulder as if expecting Aaron to walk in from the garage any moment. For the last year, Aaron had been with Yani for every family visit. Yani felt his resolve crumbling as Mom glanced back to Yani with confusion in her eyes. "Oh, Yani," she breathed as his eyes filled. She quickly stepped forward to pull Yani into a hug.

He couldn't stop the tears under Mom's comforting onslaught. The full story emerged between his gasps and sobs, mumbled into Mom's shoulder as her shirt became progressively damper.

"I know you love him, Yani, but you're right. He's not being a very good boyfriend right now, and he's going to lose you because of it. Maybe he'll come to his senses eventually, but he's hurting you, and that's unacceptable." Mom was right, but then, she usually was. "I think you need to back away from him. Make it a clean break."

Yani nodded. He pulled away from Mom and wiped his eyes on his sleeve. "I'll text Mary to see if I can sleep on her couch for a few weeks while I find a new place to live. I can ask for a transfer at work as soon as my current assignment is done."

"And you'll tell him you're splitting up the next time you see him," Mom finished firmly. "No stringing him along or worrying about it. Make it clear that the second you're back in Boston, you're going to be living two completely separate lives from now on."

Yani nodded wordlessly. It was the best way.

"Good. Now go upstairs and wash your face. Give Mary a call to let her know you're coming and send your boss an email. Then I'm going to need help with dinner, so don't take too long."

Yani nodded again before turning to obey her. He was halfway up the stairs when he heard Mom yelling down into the basement.

"Shira, get up here! I need help making dinner!"

A grin crept across Yani's face at the normality of it all. He dropped his suitcase in his room, went into the bathroom to quickly wash his face—he winced at the redness and blotches he saw in the mirror and scrubbed a little harder to make the evidence vanish faster—and then returned to his room. He pulled his phone out of his pocket and opened up a text message between him and Mary. She was the first friend he had made in college, and she was the one who had introduced Yani to Aaron through what turned out to be a very awkward blind date, and he had remained friends with her ever since.

I think Aaron and I are finished, he texted her.

Mary's reply came back a few seconds later.

OMG! No way!

A second and third text appeared almost instantaneously afterward.

Why? What did that fool do?

There were three crying faces and two angry fist emoticons added onto her last text.

It's what he's not doing that's the problem, Yani texted back.

Still no sex? she asked, coming far too close to the truth.

She was a smart lady, but Yani had also griped about Aaron not coming to bed the last time they went out for drinks together.

That isn't right. Are you really going to break up?

He's ignoring me now. We haven't had a real conversation in weeks. And yeah, no sex either.

That sux. Two yellow faces were shaking their heads back and forth at the end of this text.

But he's being an idiot. You do what you have to. Let me know how I can help.

Can I crash on your couch for a few weeks while I'm hunting for a new place to live?

Shit, I haven't told you yet! Three yellow faces smacked themselves in the forehead. *I got the job!*

That's great! Yani texted back, honestly excited for her. Then it occurred to him. *Wait, that means you're moving?!?*

The job she had gotten was located in Washington, D.C. Yani hated that she was going so far away, but he was glad she finally had a full-time job she would actually enjoy. Her current job was mostly filing, and she hated the monotony of it.

Yup. In two weeks. I just left notice with my current job. I was going to ask you over to help me pack. I can give you my couch, but I don't have a roof to go with it. Sorry.

It's okay. I'll ask someone else. Let me know when you need my manly muscles to help you move.

Please. Luke has more muscles than you. I'll let you know. Feel better!

Yani's phone fell silent, and he let out a sigh. Mary was his best hope for finding somewhere to crash. He didn't want to only move downstairs in his apartment building and stay with Luke and Brandon. For one thing, that wasn't making a clean break from Aaron, who would still be nearby. He would also be getting in the way of Luke and Brandon's personal time, which wasn't fair to them. He didn't have any other friends from the supernatural world. His college friends consisted of Mary, who was out, Tony, who lived with his serious girlfriend on the far side of Boston—too far for Yani to commute to work every day—and Ettie, who had a one-bedroom apartment she barely fit into.

His other option was to ask Bishop if he could take an empty bed in one of the dormitories in the coalition building. Bishop wouldn't say no, but at the same time, the accommodations lacked privacy. It wasn't Yani's first choice, but it would work until he was able to find a place of his own.

Yani pulled out his laptop and wrote out a quick email to Bishop asking for a place to stay and inquiring about the possibility of a transfer once they were done sorting out the werebears. He didn't go into detail.

Yani closed his computer again and turned toward his bedroom door. He paused, wanting another friendly voice in his ear, someone who understood the relationship issues as well as the supernatural ones. He pulled up a number on his phone and hit Call.

The phone rang six times before clicking over to an answering machine.

"Hey, Uncle Yakov. It's Yani. I know you're probably still sleeping, but I wanted someone to talk to. I'm going to break up with Aaron. He's gotten so lost in trying to become more powerful I hardly see him anymore. I don't like feeling so alone, and I prefer being single and alone to being in a relationship and alone. I just don't understand why magic is more important than me.

"I'm sorry I'm ranting. I think I just need a friendly ear. If you or Uncle Martin could explain what happened to Aaron, I really would appreciate it. I hope you're having a better summer than I am. We're investigating a case of a werepanda who went crazy and started attacking other animals. Let me know how the stonemasons are doing with that crumbling wall. Are you going to have someone remove all the ivy from your house before it chews through another wall? I'll be around tonight if you're able to call."

Yani hung up and sighed again. Uncle Yakov probably wouldn't be able to make heads or tails of that message. Yani had been rambling, his voice too fast for real coherency. Still, it felt good to get the story off his shoulders to someone who could understand every aspect of it. Mom was a good shoulder to cry on and her advice was sound, but Uncle Yakov lived in a magical gay relationship too. He would understand what Yani was going through at least a little better.

Without anything else to distract himself, Yani headed downstairs to help with dinner.

Mom had already finished peeling the potatoes. She was digging a cutting board out of the cabinet, but she still pointed toward the table. Shira had come upstairs at Mom's urging and was busy sorting the stack of mail that had been left there. Yani edged around Mom to pull plates out of the cabinet.

They were having steak and home fries for dinner. Dad was puttering around outside with the grill while Mom had a pan of oil heating on the stove. It didn't take long to get the table set. Just as Yani was setting down the last wineglass, Mom pulled the pan of hot oil off the fire. She carried a platter covered in paper towels with the fries nestled inside to the table, but she didn't take her seat. Shira had chosen the frozen vegetable, and she pulled it hot from the microwave and brought that to the table as well. She joined Mom standing at the nearby counter while they waited for Dad to finish with the grill. The platter of steaks was steaming as Dad brought it inside. He took his seat at the table next to Yani, and they both turned expectantly to look at Mom.

Every family's Shabbat traditions differed slightly. There was technically a set rubric for how it was done: light the candles at sundown, say the blessing over wine and challah, and eat a festive meal. Within those strictures, however, families could and did add their own flair.

Solemnly, Mom lit the two candles in Gramma's old silver candlesticks, waited patiently to make sure both wicks were caught, and then sang the short prayer. Shira stood at Mom's side, but once she was a bat mitzvah, she would light her own candles with Mom. The candles stated that Shabbat had officially started. For most Jews, Shabbat—Saturday—was a day of prayer and connection to G-d. They weren't allowed to work or do anything that required effort except for praying. Yani's family didn't always attend synagogue, but they celebrated with a fancy meal, all the traditions, and by having a relaxing Saturday.

Dad poured the wine while Mom and Shira took their seats. Shira only got a finger's width since she wasn't a bat mitzvah yet. Yani had gotten half a glass after his bar mitzvah, basically just a little more than a shot, until he'd turned twenty-one and could legally drink. Yani sang the prayer over wine and then everyone drank. Next, and last, was challah. Shira uncovered the two braided loaves of bread, folded the fancy cloth cover, and set it to the side. Once that was done, the whole family joined in singing the prayer. Dad cut the challah into slices when they were done.

Yani ate his slice of challah, then picked up his grapefruit spoon and cut into the wedge of cantaloupe Mom had prepared for everyone as an appetizer. He was holding back tears again, but this time he didn't think anyone noticed.

Shabbat dinner to Yani meant a return to normalcy. Everything was still exactly the same as it had been when he was a child. Aaron hadn't had a chance to imprint himself into this aspect of Yani's life; his absence didn't grate on Yani for the first time in weeks. The relief was intense. It would be short-lived, Yani knew. On Monday, he had to return to work and Aaron. Still, for this brief time, Yani could let all the pain go and just enjoy.

"So, Olivia had her baby," Dad said once everyone had swallowed.

"She did!" Mom gasped. "When did you find out? That's two now, right? One more to go!"

Olivia was Dad's niece. She lived in Chicago with the rest of Dad's family. When he met Mom in college at Syracuse University, he had made the decision to stay in the East so Mom could remain with her family. Yani had met Olivia a few times, although he hadn't seen her since her wedding a few years back.

"If she decides to have more." Dad disagreed. "I found out this morning at work. It's a boy, so the bris is coming up. I was thinking about flying out."

"You have to go. I'll see if I can get off work," Mom replied immediately. She loved kids, Yani knew, and she also firmly believed that every Jewish family needed to have at least three children: one to replace yourself, one to replace your spouse, and one to replace someone murdered in the Holocaust. Mom had had trouble having more kids after Yani. He didn't remember much of it since he was so young, but he did remember the jubilation and shock when the doctors announced Shira was going to make it when he'd been ten years old.

The conversation continued without Yani's input. Appetizer plates were put aside, and the steak, potatoes, and green beans were served. Yani let the normalcy continue to wash over him until he finally relaxed.

*

Yani was miserable. He'd wiped his sweaty forehead on his sleeve fifteen minutes ago, and the cloth was still damp. Water didn't evaporate in the Adirondack Mountains: it fell from the sky and then stayed for days. It had rained two days ago, but drops of water still fell from the leaves overhead, hitting Yani's head and adding to his generally soggy state. Honestly, it was horrible. Yani had no idea why people wanted to live up here.

The roof of the guest cabin Yani, Aaron, Brandon, and Luke were using was covered in thick moss and lichen. There were mushrooms growing in abundance as well, and the scent of must and mold overtook everything. Even the pleasant smell of pine was lost amid the damp.

"We need to talk about today," Brandon said as he walked into the living room.

The cabin they had been given wasn't large. It had one bedroom in the back, with two sets of bunk beds, a bathroom they all shared, and a combination living room and kitchen in the front. Yani was sitting in one of the armchairs. Aaron looked up from the book he had been engrossed in, blinking owlishly at the room around him as his attention was finally pulled back into the real world.

"What's the plan?" Aaron asked. He actually closed the book and set it aside. Yani thought he might go into shock.

Yani had also apparently turned into a sarcastic bitch over the last few hours. He took a deep breath and forced his unhappiness aside. They were here for a job, and once that was done, Yani wouldn't have to see Aaron ever again. Bishop had emailed him back over the weekend, reassuring Yani there was a position open for him and a bed he could use when he returned to coalition headquarters.

Luke joined them a few minutes later. His hair was still damp, although it was difficult to tell if that was because he had just gotten out of the shower or because it wasn't drying in this humidity. Luke was one of the most handsome men Yani had ever met, which made sense, given the fact that he was an incubus. His cheekbones were model high, his lips plump, and his eyes an alluring shade of blue. He and Yani had dated a few years ago, so Yani knew just how enticing Luke could be, but one look at Brandon had cemented Luke's attentions forever.

Luke's mating bond with Brandon was amazingly strong. He joined Brandon on the couch and snuggled close.

"So far, what we know is that a werepanda named Maki suddenly went crazy," Brandon began. "She killed four wild bears before the local population of werebears caught up with her. She attempted to kill them too. Once they subdued her, the madness apparently subsided. She came to the coalition placidly enough and is currently locked away in one of the coalition's cells."

"We need to search the woods around her house and investigate the bodies of the dead bears to see if we can find out what made her go crazy," Luke continued. "We should also search her house to see if we can find any illegal substances that could have caused her behavior."

"We need to see if she caused the madness, or if someone attacked her instead," Brandon finished.

Yani nodded in agreement, but he couldn't help feeling upset by how the meeting was going. Just a few months ago, Aaron would have been the one who knew every aspect of the case and would direct them in their investigation. Now Aaron was barely listening to their overview. His eyes kept straying over to where he had put his book aside. Yani couldn't say for certain whether anything Brandon and Luke were saying was getting to Aaron's brain.

"What did Maki say when you spoke with her?" Yani asked. He had missed that conversation because he'd had to catch the bus home.

"We couldn't actually speak with her," Brandon said with a sharp frown over at Aaron. "She's apparently stuck in panda form, and when we asked Aaron to come take a look, he agreed and then never bothered."

"You never asked me that," Aaron replied immediately, apparently following enough of their conversation to know he was being accused of negligence.

"I asked you, and Grandpa asked you," Brandon disagreed. "You're so damned stuck in your stupid books you didn't even notice we were there!"

"It's important that I learn this!" Aaron said, sounding incensed that someone would call his books stupid. "My magic is what saved us the last time we confronted Cain, and I need to get better so I can defeat him when we finally find him again."

"Yet you can't be bothered to spin a little spell to try to figure out why a werepanda is stuck in panda form," Luke replied with a sneer. "Some magic. Besides, if I remember correctly, it was Yani who escaped Cain, rescued us, figured out what was powering the djinni so you could disable it, and found us a way out of Cain's lair. You just tossed some magic around. Without Yani, you would be Cain's puppet, and the rest of us would be dead."

"Come on, Luke," Brandon cut in. "Let's focus on this case now. We can fight later."

"No, we're going to fight now," Luke replied. "I don't want this entire investigation to be hobbled because Aaron's head is stuck too far up his ass!"

"What are you talking about?" Aaron snarled back. There was a touch of magic in his voice, and Yani could see it swirl around him briefly in a rope of sparkles before Aaron got control over it again.

"Aaron, why don't you tell us what Yani told us in the car? See if you were actually listening, or if you were too busy with your magic to bother listening to your own boyfriend," Luke said, pointedly turning to look at Aaron as he spoke.

Their conversation was spiraling out of control faster than Yani could believe. All four of them had been best friends for years now, happy to work together even in the worst circumstances because they always had each other's backs. Not so much now, apparently.

"You might as well tell him," Brandon added with a heavy sigh.

"I asked Bishop for a transfer," Yani finally said. Aaron needed to hear this, even if chances were he would vanish back into his book instead of saying anything to try to keep Yani with them. He hadn't in the car when Yani had told all three of them his plans, which had hurt much more than Yani had believed it could. "When we return to Boston, I'll be working somewhere else. He's also given me a bed in one of the dormitories there while I look for a new apartment."

"What's wrong with our apartment right now?" Aaron asked. He looked honestly confused—the first forthright emotion Yani had seen from him in months. His eyes weren't glazed and vacant as he focused on a book or spell. Instead, they were looking directly at Yani.

"The problem," Yani replied with a shake of his head, "is that you're there. Aaron, I'm moving out, and we're breaking up."

The look of utter devastation that crossed Aaron's face almost made Yani want to retract his words. However, a brief moment of lucidity wasn't enough to make up for the last few months of absence.

"Why?" Aaron forced out.

Yani sighed. "Because you don't know why. You've been so oblivious for so long, Aaron, and I've had enough." Aaron looked utterly bewildered, and Yani couldn't stay in the same room with him any longer. A very large part of Yani, the part that still truly and deeply loved Aaron, wanted to rush over to Aaron's side and apologize. He wanted so badly to give Aaron yet another chance, but there had been plenty of those over the last few months. It took practically everything Yani had to stand and head to the door while ignoring Aaron, whose mouth was opening and closing, though no words escaped.

As the door closed behind Yani, he heard Aaron finally speak. "What did I do?" he asked, and the tears Yani had been holding back vanished almost immediately. Aaron had been so sucked up into his own little world that he really had no idea what the last few months had been like for Yani. Nothing Yani had said or done had managed to penetrate the shield Aaron had erected around himself.

"When was the last time you and Yani had sex?" Brandon asked sharply. "When was the last time you sat down to dinner with him or asked him about his day? How about even having a basic conversation? You don't have to answer that," Brandon continued scathingly, "because I already know the answer is you have no idea. It's been months, Aaron."

Yani walked down the steps, unable to listen any longer. Well-marked dirt paths connected all the houses in the werebears' little village. Yani followed one aimlessly, climbing the steep and sometimes rocky slope without care of where it might lead him. He kept his eyes open, of course. Not only was he in the middle of an investigation, but Maki might have gotten involved in something weird. The last thing he wanted to do was blindly stumble into trouble just because personal issues were distracting him.

He didn't see anything out of the ordinary, though. Yani's powers were in his eyes, the ability to see magic and through illusion. He had been born with it, and when Cain had captured Yani, Cain had chosen to enhance it first before attempting to steal it. There wasn't much in the supernatural world that Yani couldn't see.

"I thought I smelled something different in the woods," a sibilant voice said from behind a nearby tree. The owner of the voice stepped onto the path, blocking Yani's way. "I smelled wolf, slut, magic, and you. I've never smelled anything like you before."

Yani had to blink a few times before he was absolutely certain of what his normal sight was telling him and the differences his magical sight imparted. The man's skin was dark black—not what Yani would consider a human color, but it seemed to work for him. Yani could see the black skin was actually tiny scales, each no bigger than his pinky nail. The man's tongue was forked in Yani's special sight.

"You're not the first person to tell me that," Yani replied warily.

The man was tall and his dark eyes intent as he studied Yani like a mystery he was determined to solve. His tongue flickered out of his mouth like a snake tasting the air. "There is something very strange emanating from you. I smell a regular human that has been steeped in magic. Yet the smell of magic has begun to fade from you.

Additionally, I smell the wicked taint of blood magic. You are very intriguing, I have to say. Please, call me Khan. What should I call you?"

Yani could only think of two people named Khan. Genghis Khan, the warlord from ancient times who had conquered much of the world, and Khan, the evil superhuman being from the *Star Trek* TV shows and movies who was bent on eliminating the human race. The name did not bode well.

"My name is Yani," Yani replied, unable to not be polite.

"A Hebrew diminutive of Ian," Khan murmured thoughtfully. "How quaint. I like you, Yani. You interest me, and not much has kept my interest for quite a long time."

"Is that a good thing?" Yani asked, hoping he wasn't about to open a can of worms. This was a community of bears where something bad had happened, and now someone who most definitely wasn't a bear had appeared. That was quite a coincidence.

Khan opened his mouth, but before he could answer, someone let out a low growl behind Yani.

"Go back to your hole in the ground, Khan," Randy snarled. He was one of the werebears Yani had been introduced to yesterday evening. Randy seemed unhappy about everything, both growling about Yani and his friends invading their woods and demanding that Maki be executed for her crimes at once. He was the most vocal about how disappointed he was that justice for the slain bears had been remanded to the coalition.

"These are my woods as well, bear-kin, and I have just as much right to walk through them as you." Khan sounded utterly unconcerned about Randy's ire, yet his tongue flickered in and out of his mouth, like a nervous reaction, at least twice. Randy didn't appear to notice, so Yani felt it was safe to assume that only he could see it.

Randy sneered but didn't answer. He looked at Yani instead. "Stay away from the snake if you know what's good for you." He turned and stomped his way back into the woods.

"It appears I have overstayed my welcome." Khan sighed dramatically. "I suppose I should go back to my hole in the ground, as he so welcomingly put it, but I will see you again, Yani."

Khan walked into the woods in the opposite direction Randy had gone. Yani was alone in the woods again, but he was feeling considerably better. He followed the path back to the cabin. Brandon and Luke were waiting outside.

"Ready to go?" Luke asked kindly.

Yani nodded. "Which way is the scene?"

Brandon pointed down yet another path. "We're just waiting to see if Aaron's planning to join us today. He said he's just going to put his book down and be right out." Brandon's frown said he didn't believe Aaron, but they were going to wait five more minutes to give Aaron a chance anyway.

Shockingly, the door opened a few seconds later, and Aaron stepped outside. He wouldn't look at Yani as he moved around them all and started walking down the path.

"There is magic in the air, but it's weird," Aaron explained. "Some of the magic feels like bear, some feels like a very odd snake, and underneath it all is an undertone of blood magic."

"I think I can explain the snake," Yani said. "I just ran into a guy calling himself Khan. He was hiding black scales and a forked tongue underneath a glamour of some sort."

"Weird. I wonder what he is," Brandon said.

"Sounds like a dragon," Aaron replied immediately. "They're very rare and very powerful. I'm shocked one would live up here." Aaron knew a lot more than just Kabbalah. He specialized in simply knowing everything that needed to be known about the magical community. It was a hard reminder that when Aaron was present, both physically and mentally, he was their most important asset. "I wonder what he wanted?"

"He said he wanted to know what we were doing here. Came to check out the new smells in the woods," Yani explained. "He could smell what Cain did to me."

"Superior senses, superior strength, and amazing at magic. Or so I read," Aaron added. "I wonder if he knows what happened to our suspect."

"We don't even know what happened to our suspect, since we couldn't actually talk to her," Brandon growled.

"I'm sorry, okay? It won't happen again." Aaron did look contrite and upset. His shoulders were slumped slightly, and he was frowning. He kept looking over at Yani as if expecting Yani to forgive him and forget their problems. Yani wanted to, but a half hour of lucidity did not make up for months of nothing. As long as Yani kept reminding himself of that fact, he would be able to remain firm on his decision to leave Aaron.

They reached the clearing where Maki had allegedly savaged the bears and paused. The carcasses had been removed before they could bloat and start reeking, but the stench of blood still permeated the area. Black flies flew in abundance over the blood-soaked grass, buzzing and moving so quickly that Yani couldn't actually see through them to the grass below.

Yani thought he saw a black cloud hovering low to the ground, but it was obscured by the flies a second later. Brandon was the first to actually step into the clearing. He sniffed the air cautiously. His werewolf nose could detect minute differences and give them forewarning about any dangers ahead.

"There is something weird here. It almost smells rotten." He took another step closer, still sniffing. Yani concentrated on the flies, trying to see if that black cloud was really there or if it was just another swarm of flies.

Suddenly the flies shifted to one side of the clearing, and Yani saw it. It was dark and evil looking, like the bottom of a funnel cloud just before a tornado descended to earth.

"Get back!" Yani yelled at the same time Brandon let out a loud snarl. Yani spun to look just as Brandon started changing shape. Bones snapped, and a slow groan came from Brandon.

"What is it?" Luke asked desperately as he hovered between stepping forward to see if he could help and running back to a safe distance. "Brandon, what's wrong?"

"There's a sort of cloud hidden among the flies," Yani explained quickly, watching Brandon closely as he finished shifting forms and stood on four paws. He was a handsome wolf with thick blond fur. He was also considerably larger than a wolf in the wild might be.

Brandon slowly turned toward them, a low rumble emanating from his chest. There wasn't any recognition in his eyes as he stared at them with his fangs bared.

"I don't see any flies," Luke whispered. He was staring back at Brandon as if he couldn't quite believe that no one was home. "Brandon, what do you smell?"

Brandon let out another low snarl, crouched, and then sprang at them with his claws extended.

"Shit!" Aaron swore as he ducked. Yani backed up until he hit a tree. Brandon went after Luke first, growling and snarling as he charged. Just before they collided with what Yani knew would have been terrible force, Luke vanished. He reappeared next to Yani, panting for breath. Brandon spun, dug his claws into the ground, and sprang again. Straight at Yani.

"Don't!" Aaron yelled. Magic flared, and Yani could feel its strength. If it hit Brandon, he would die and Yani might get caught in the crossfire.

"Fools," Khan said as he slid easily between Yani, Brandon, and Aaron's spell. He held out his hands to each side. The spell hit his left hand and faded away impotently with a shower of sparks. Brandon ran straight into Khan's other hand and bounced backward. He snarled again and charged, only to be sent flying away a second time.

Khan began mumbling under his breath as Brandon continued to charge over and over again, only to be repelled over and over. It was thoughtless, and Yani knew that if Brandon were in his right mind, he would be mortified to have lost control so easily. Brandon had been working so hard to become an alpha, which meant he should have been able to keep his wolf constrained under any circumstances. That he had utterly lost control meant they weren't up against an ordinary spell.

Aaron was also muttering to himself, but he had stopped focusing on Brandon and was instead staring intently into the cloud of flies.

Brandon ran toward Khan as Khan's voice rose to a crescendo. A spell flashed from Khan's outstretched hand and hit Brandon, who slumped to the ground unconscious. Luke immediately rushed around Khan to kneel at Brandon's side, gently petting Brandon's fur.

Aaron's muttering also became louder, quickly forming into actual words. At least, Yani assumed they were real words, since they were in a mishmash of Middle Eastern languages both modern and ancient and Yani could just barely pick out the few in modern Hebrew. The flies started dropping to the ground, vanishing before they could touch the bloody grass. Yani could see the black cloud clearly, and it made him press backward against the tree again.

The cloud snarled like Brandon had a moment ago: wild and completely uncontrolled. It turned to Aaron so slowly that Yani understood why it had used the flies for camouflage. Aaron's chanting grew in intensity as the cloud inched closer. It seemed to be working because the cloud slowed to a stop.

"I was right to come investigate the new smells in the woods," Khan said as he stepped around Brandon and Luke and headed toward the cloud. "I haven't been this entertained in at least a century." He stuck one hand deep into the cloud, which made the cloud shudder. The fistful he pulled free pulsed in Yani's sight like a beating heart. Khan brought it to his mouth and took a large bite.

Aaron fell silent as the cloud dissipated harmlessly while Khan continued to enjoy his impromptu snack.

"Is Brandon okay?" Luke asked. His fingers were buried in the ruff around Brandon's neck.

"He will be sane when he wakes," Khan replied between bites. "Whether he is able to return to human shape will depend greatly on the strength of his will."

"Like Maki," Luke said. "She's still stuck in panda form."

"This must have been what she ran into," Yani agreed.

"Not ran into," Khan disagreed.

"It was placed here," Aaron finished. "I'll bet Maki's cabin is just down that path." He pointed across the clearing toward where the path continued onward into the woods.

"You would be correct," Arnold, the leader of the wearbears, said as he stepped out of the woods on the path Yani, Aaron, Luke, and Brandon had just come from. "I came as soon as I heard the commotion. What happened?" He caught sight of Khan and stilled in shock. "Hello, Khan."

"Arnold," Khan replied stiffly. "I ate the curse that attacked your panda and this wolf here. You are lucky more of your sleuth were not afflicted."

"This is a fairly remote part of our woods. Only our guest house and Maki's home are located down here."

"So it was placed here specifically to attack Maki," Aaron guessed.

Arnold grimaced. "That's why I called the coalition. Maki has always kept to herself and never caused problems before. It was extremely out of character for her to lose control like she did."

"Who has the power to create a spell and leave it to hurt Maki?" Aaron asked.

"Khan does," Arnold said thoughtfully, with an apologetic shrug toward Khan.

"He is correct, but I was not the one who created such a malevolent spell." Khan frowned down at the hand he had used to tear out the heart of the cloud. "This spell was uniquely evil."

Yani shared a look with Aaron and Luke, wondering if Cain had finally returned. It had been years since they had escaped him, and there hadn't been any sign of him since. He was always on their minds, of course, but despite all their searching, he had continued to remain elusive. Had Cain finally made his move?

"It also tastes like bear. I would hazard a guess that one of your sleuth was the last to handle the spell before it was activated." Khan looked certain of his words.

That didn't make Arnold happy, but he nodded anyway. "Thank you for all your help."

"I had fun," Khan replied flippantly, then turned toward Yani. "If you need me for anything else, Arnold knows where to find me." He turned and walked off into the woods.

"Let's go back to the guest house." Arnold sighed. "I'll explain what I can, and hopefully you'll be able to find a way to figure out which of my bears is involved with something evil."

Arnold looked at Luke for permission before bending down to get his hands underneath Brandon's body. Brandon was heavy as a wolf, easily over two hundred pounds, but Arnold lifted him into the air as if Brandon were a mere feather. Bears were one of the physically strongest of the were-species. Arnold led the way down the path, retracing their route, without looking the least bit winded. Luke trotted along at Brandon's side, looking anxious.

The guesthouse appeared quickly enough. Luke opened the door so Arnold could maneuver Brandon inside, and he set Brandon down on a nearby rug. Everyone else filed into the living room, edging around Brandon to take seats. Once they were all settled into the chairs and couches, Arnold sighed heavily again.

"Maki made her home with us, but we never made her feel welcome. We're mostly black bears, and she's a panda. Including her in the sleuth always felt weird, to be honest. She never complained. She liked the solitude, I think, and the fact that we left her alone for the most part."

"For the most part?" Luke asked, echoing Yani's own thoughts. It sounded like Arnold was trying to come up with excuses as to why Maki had lived a lonely and isolated life among those as similar to her own kind as she was likely to find in the entire United States.

"There were one or two of us who heckled her, but it never became violent, and she never complained about it to me. She knew she could always come to me if she needed anything."

"Was Randy one of them?" Yani asked, remembering Randy's ire at him from earlier that day.

"He was one of the more vocal ones," Arnold confirmed. "And he was very against my contacting the coalition instead of meting out justice immediately. I'm glad that I didn't take his advice now that we know someone lured Maki into a trap."

"We need to talk to all of those hecklers," Luke instructed.

"I'll have them come here this afternoon. I'll escort them myself if need be," Arnold said.

They sat in silence for a few moments longer. Yani was trying to think of any more questions to ask Arnold while they had his undivided attention, but he couldn't come up with anything. His mind was spinning with too much information. Maki being tricked, Khan being a dragon, Brandon possibly being stuck in wolf form, and Aaron.

He was still in shock over the spell Aaron had fired at Brandon. Yes, Brandon hadn't known what he was doing, and both Yani and Luke had been in grave danger, but Aaron's spell could have killed all three of them. It was beyond reckless and stupid, yet Aaron had done it anyway.

What had all that studying been for if the first bit of magic Yani had seen Aaron do in months was that horrible?

"I can't believe one of my bears would willingly set a spell like that and then leave it once their intended target had been taken out!" Arnold growled suddenly, breaking the silence. "Any one of my bears could have easily walked into the spell just like your wolf did, and if they were stronger than Maki, some of my sleuth could have died. We were barely able to contain her with minimal injury."

"We can't rule out the fact that Maki might have set the spell herself," Luke cut in. "Maybe she was accidentally caught in it when she was placing it in that clearing in the hopes of afflicting some of her hecklers as they were heading to her cabin."

That was also very possible. Yani couldn't keep working under the assumption that Maki was innocent. There were always deeper facets to any investigation. He needed to keep an open mind so he didn't inadvertently miss something. If they hadn't continued to investigate past the crimes the leprechaun had committed, they never would have found out that the miller's family was guilty as well.

"We'll need to search her place," Luke finished.

"You did tell me that earlier," Arnold reminded them. He dug in his pocket for a second and produced a key. He handed it to Aaron, who was sitting closest. "I'll need that back when you're done." He stood and nodded to them before turning and leaving the cabin as if his giving them the key was a dismissal.

Yani looked at the key in Aaron's hand and held back a grimace. Luke needed to stay behind with Brandon to explain what had happened when Brandon woke up. That left Yani and Aaron to head over to Maki's cabin. Except, Aaron stood up and headed back into the bedroom.

"I'll get the key and head over to Maki's place." Yani sighed. He stood to follow Aaron, trying hard to ignore Luke's look of pity as Yani walked past.

Aaron had settled onto the bottom bunk of the closest bed. His ever-present book was in his hands, but it was closed and he was staring down at it.

"What have I been doing, Yani?" Aaron whispered. His voice was so low that Yani had to lean closer to hear him. "I almost killed everyone in that clearing with a spell that should have only frozen Brandon in place."

"I have no idea what you've been up to. We haven't spoken in months, Aaron. I have no idea what you've been studying or what might have gone wrong."

"There's something wrong with me. I need to figure out what it is before I really do hurt someone." Aaron felt along the spine of the book until his fingers found the bookmark shoved between the pages. Yani stepped forward and slapped his hand down on the cover before Aaron could open it.

"Here's a thought," Yani hissed, incensed that Aaron's first reaction to having a problem was to open that *facacta* book again. "The last time we spoke, you weren't having any problems with your magic. The only thing that's changed since then was you got so engrossed in this damned book you shut out the rest of the world."

"That's not..." Aaron paused, staring down at Yani's hand on the cover of the book. "My studies shouldn't have a negative effect on my magic!"

"One of the first things Myobu Sensei taught me when she took me as her student was that balance was important. Aaron, you've abandoned everything except what you can learn from a book. You've chased me away, you've alienated your friends, and you've left behind everything else you used to enjoy." The reminder hurt wounds that were still raw and bleeding, but at the same time, he couldn't stand by and not offer any help. Aaron deserved that much when he was struggling to make sense of his life without Yani in it. Their relationship had meant so much to Yani for so long that he shouldn't walk away from Aaron when Aaron looked so devastated. Yet Yani knew he had to. They weren't dating any longer, and Mom had said a clean break would be best.

Yani leaned over Aaron to grab the key sitting on the bedspread.

"I'm going to have a look around Maki's place. You need to figure out what happened to make you so lost."

Yani stood and walked out of the bedroom. Luke was curled up on the rug around Brandon, crooning softly to him as Yani walked past and out the door.

There was water dripping from the trees overhead, even though it hadn't rained recently. Apparently even the trees were sweating in the constant humidity.

It only took a few minutes to walk up the hill to Maki's home. When Yani walked through the clearing, he didn't see a single sign of a black fly or evil cloud.

Maki's home was a small cabin tucked under a canopy of low-hanging pines. Yani let himself inside with the key and shut the door behind him. He stood in the entryway for a moment to take in the completely unexpected décor. Every other building Yani had been in had heavy wooden furniture and a general air of decay caused by the almost constant dampness. Maki had instead gone Japanese, and the building smelled and looked clean and fresh. There wasn't mold growing in the corners of the ceiling, which must have taken a ton of effort, and the light, flowery scent filling the air was such a pleasant change that Yani just wanted to breathe it in for a few moments.

The cabin was split into three distinct areas: a main room, a bedroom, and a bathroom off to one side. The couches in the main room were delicate, with cherry blossom flowers printed onto the upholstery. She had a small bonsai tree on the kitchen table surrounded by modern chrome appliances. Three kabuki masks hung on the walls. He found an air scent plugged into the wall next to the fridge, which explained why the room smelled so nice. Most significantly, Yani didn't see any sign of magic.

Magic had a sort of sparkle to it that ordinary objects lacked. A pot that was spelled to not burn the food inside, for example, would flare in Yani's sight the second he looked at it. Even the very dark magic from the clearing had its own special tint to it, one which told Yani immediately that it was magical in nature. There wasn't anything magical in origin anywhere in the main room. Yani opened every drawer and cabinet and found absolutely nothing with magic in it. Whoever had been willing and able to place the spell in the clearing was well versed in magic, much more so than the evidence said Maki was.

Yani finished with the main room and checked the bathroom next. He found the same result there and headed to Maki's bedroom to finish the search.

Maki had a large bed set up against one wall. It and the small nightstand next to it were the only furniture in the room. There was a walk-in closet off to one side, but Yani's attention was immediately fixed on the small drawer in the nightstand. The sparkle of magic was heavily concentrated there.

Opening the drawer when he didn't have any backup with him was probably stupid, but Yani reached out anyway.

There were two objects inside that held magic. The one on top was a delicate necklace. It looked old, the gold tarnished and worn from many hands holding it through the generations. The charm was a pink cherry blossom, the same blossom as on the couches in the main room, except this one looked like a sprig had been taken directly from the tree only an hour earlier. The pink gems appeared to be diamonds to Yani's inexperienced eye. He could see magic in those stones.

Nothing about the necklace looked or felt malevolent to Yani. It felt like life and happiness, but as Yani watched, a black centipede slithered out from underneath. The bug was evil, exactly like the flies, and it caught sight of Yani almost immediately. Wings flared on the bug's back, and it literally hissed at Yani, who quickly slammed the drawer shut.

That hadn't been the necklace. There was definitely something else in that drawer, and the necklace was hiding it. Yani stayed far away from the nightstand as he searched the rest of the room, but there was nothing else with magic in it that he could find.

Yani walked back out into the main room and pulled his cell phone from his pocket to call Luke.

"You found something," Luke said immediately when the call connected.

"Yes, but I don't think I should be touching it," Yani replied. "Is Aaron available? And how's Brandon doing?"

"Brandon woke up and is lucid. He can't change back just yet, but Aaron came out of hiding to take a closer look at the spell."

"Okay, I get it!" Yani heard Aaron yell. "I fucked up. Stop reminding me."

"I could use Aaron here when he's finished with Brandon. I found two spells. One is on a necklace, but the magic feels good and it's masking something else that is very, very bad."

Yani heard the rustle as Luke pulled the phone away from his ear and the murmur of voices talking beyond the microphone. Without Aaron yelling, Yani couldn't make out the words. Luke returned a moment later.

"Aaron says give him ten minutes to finish looking at Brandon. We'll all come over then to have a look around too."

Yani opened his mouth to agree, but he never got the words out. He felt the explosion before he heard it. A thump hit him in the chest and the ground shook, and then his ears rang with the booming crash. Yani fell to the floor with his hands instinctively pressed over his ears in protection.

"Yani! Yani, are you okay?"

The phone was still in his hand, and Luke's frantic voice caused Yani to sit up and clutch the phone to his ear.

"I'm fine," Yani wheezed, trying to regain his breath as quickly as possible after that thud. "Are you guys okay?"

"Yeah. We think that was in the mountains." Yani heard a squeak of a door opening. "Yeah, I can see smoke over the trees."

Yani hurried outside Maki's cabin and immediately saw what Luke was describing. Black smoke drifted over the trees higher up the mountain. What Yani didn't see was the red and orange of fire. It might have been obscured by the trees, but Yani doubted it. An explosion as big as Yani had felt should have leveled the trees and caused flames to fill the entire forest.

"Aaron says something suppressed the fire," Luke said into the phone, echoing exactly where Yani's own thoughts were headed.

"Khan lives somewhere up there, right?" Yani asked.

The smoke was drifting closer and appeared to be taking on a much more distinct shape. Wings coalesced first, and then a massive body solidified out of the smoke. The dragon roared, shaking the mountain again as it descended.

"Yeah, I think so," Luke replied, sounding slightly out of breath.

The dragon was magnificent-looking, and Yani knew Luke had a weakness for beauty. He wouldn't act on it because he was tied tightly and happily to Brandon, but that didn't mean he couldn't appreciate the sight as much as Yani did. Each scale looked like a perfectly cut and shined opal, sparkling brilliantly as the sunlight reflected off it. The wings were huge and leathery. They only pumped twice in the air, powerful down strokes that flattened the trees below, before the wings folded into the body and the dragon dove.

Khan was coming straight at Yani, and there was no way he could run and escape in time. Even if he went back inside Maki's house, the dragon would still catch him. It could tear the roof off with its long talons without any trouble.

Yani only had a few seconds to make a decision, which wasn't nearly long enough when the hard scales and pointed teeth were coming straight at him. He froze instead, unable to choose, and felt the heavy wash of air as the wings were flung open again directly over his head.

Khan stopped in midair, so Yani was peeking out between the fingers covering his head when Khan spoke.

"I wish to lodge a formal complaint against the ursa clan with the coalition. Will you hear my case?" Khan's voice was deeper, and Yani could hear the crackle of flames, giving it a sinister edge. It made his body and mind suddenly unfreeze as the memories of a different being made of fire resurfaced. This time, Yani knew he had to run, had to escape the fire before he was utterly consumed. The burn on his arm flared with pain.

"We will hear your complaint," Luke called as he and the rest of Yani's group hurried to Yani's side.

Yani took a deep, stuttering breath and let it out in a hard whoosh. He repeated the process, and the illusory pain on his arm vanished as if it had never been there.

One fear—the dragon flying down to kill him—had triggered his ongoing fear of uncontrolled flame. Yani had better control of the *meshugaas*, of the issues he had been struggling to overcome, than this. He had worked with a therapist and his sensei to overcome the shiver of fear even just seeing a candle flame had brought in him. It had been months since he had frozen like this, and he had thought he was getting better. That clearly wasn't the case. It was jarring to realize just how much his fear was still able to control him.

"My complaint is thus: I smelled one of the ursa clan near my home, invading the territory I have carefully marked and declared solely my own. When I went to investigate, I was cruelly attacked by a spell much like the one I had eaten earlier today. I believe one of the ursa attempted to assassinate me."

"Would you recognize the scent if you smelled it again?" Aaron asked.

"I would," Khan replied without hesitation.

"Let's gather the bears then," Luke finished.

Khan's gigantic body began to shrink, revealing trees below his legs that had been crushed by his landing. His human form emerged a moment later.

Yani took one last deep breath and forced the last of his fear away. The feel of the cold sweat on his skin was vile, but it wasn't any different to the continuing dampness that surrounded him.

"No need to gather them," Arnold said as he jogged toward them. "John already confessed to leaving both spells. I have him confined."

"You're sure it was him?" Yani asked sharply. This was far too convenient.

Arnold sighed heavily. "Honestly, no. He's not a strong personality, and I think it would be far too easy for someone to convince him to act on their behalf."

"You want to pretend to believe John," Aaron guessed. "Which should keep the actual culprit from running."

"We can do a more thorough search through Maki's house," Yani added. "I found another dark spell in her bedroom. It was hidden pretty well, and I want to know if she did it or if someone's trying to frame her."

Brandon let out a short bark and pawed pointedly at his nose.

"Between the werewolf and myself, we should be able to suss out the culprit," Khan agreed. He was fully clothed, but the black scales along his bared arms looked darker and more prominent than Yani remembered.

"Since we're here, let's have a look at Maki's house and then go see what John has to say," Luke decided. He ran his fingers through the fur on Brandon's back as he spoke. Brandon arched up into his touch with a happy rumble.

They all turned and trooped back into Maki's house. Khan smelled faintly like smoke, Yani noticed as Khan brushed past him to get into the house. Yani held back. He didn't want to influence anyone by pointing out what he had seen.

"I do believe I have missed the most interesting part of this scuffle," Khan murmured as Yani neared him. He was looking at Yani through lowered brows. "You have yet to see me as a human, have you?" It was a statement more than a question, but the tilt to his head told Yani that Khan was waiting for an answer.

His eyes-that-see wasn't something he liked to advertise, but Khan clearly already knew the truth.

"I can see your scales," Yani confirmed.

"How curious. That ability is something common to those touched by vampires that requires a genetic predisposition. Who in your family had the condition prior to you?"

That was an interesting question. Uncle Yakov would have told Yani if he had any powers beyond a vampire's. He couldn't think of anyone else in his family who had gotten close enough to the supernatural world to know.

Except for Gramma, but she had taken the story of Uncle Yakov to her deathbed. He doubted she would have told them. And, of course, the Holocaust had decimated the rest of his family.

"The Nazis killed too much of my family to be certain who had it before me." His dad's family was far too normal for his powers to have come from them, so Yani didn't even consider them.

"Ah, of course. My apologies," Khan said with a polite bow of his head. "I have overstepped myself. It is simply far too refreshing to find someone I am unable to hide myself from." The pointed teeth he revealed with his grin didn't exactly reassure Yani, yet at the same time, the real joy in the shine of his eyes made Yani smile back. "Come. I can smell the dark magic, and I want to intercept it before your fool of a mage tries to kill you all yet again."

Aaron wasn't a fool, although Yani couldn't be certain how much of his kneejerk reaction was caused by his lingering feelings for Aaron. It was also undeniable that Aaron was the smartest and most accomplished of their group. However, Aaron was having trouble controlling his magic, so maybe Khan was right to be worried.

The rest of the group was in the bedroom already when Yani and Khan joined them. Brandon was sniffing along the bedside drawer, so Aaron reached out and pulled it open. Yani braced himself, but nothing happened.

"This necklace is very old," Aaron said immediately. "It's good magic, though, probably a good luck charm meant to help the wearer. It looks Asian in origin, probably Japanese." He hadn't reached out to touch it yet, possibly sensing the danger lurking underneath. Yani was about to warn them, but the winged centipede beat him to it. The dark creature jumped out from underneath the necklace and flew directly at Aaron.

Khan beat everyone there. His fingers clamped around the centipede in midair, and he held it up to his face.

"I've used quite a bit of energy today stopping the bomb from killing me and destroying my mountain. This should replenish me nicely." With that said, he opened his mouth and popped the bug inside. The centipede vanished with a crunch as Khan chewed.

Aaron frowned at Khan but didn't protest. Instead, he pulled a cloth from his pocket that sparkled slightly in Yani's vision. Aaron used the cloth to pick up the necklace. He wrapped the necklace carefully and then used a second cloth to dig through the drawer. It didn't take him long to find the centipede's nest, a small black box tucked innocuously between a hairbrush and a paperback book. Aaron was quick to wrap it in the second cloth.

"I'll take these back and have a closer look," Aaron explained as he closed the drawer. "It's pretty damning to find evidence of dark magic in her bedroom."

"It's too coincidental," Luke disagreed immediately, echoing Yani's own thoughts. "The spell in the forest clearing had been well formed. That wasn't something someone stupid enough to leave evidence in her own bedside table would do."

Brandon barked in agreement. He touched his nose with one paw and then pointed toward the drawer.

"The wolf is correct," Khan interpreted. "While the scent of the panda fills the air, I also detect the bear that attacked me. The wolf and I should be able to pick out exactly who left behind that bug to ensure the panda was executed for her perceived crimes."

"We should talk to John next, see if he smells right," Yani added.

It didn't take long to close up Maki's house and follow Arnold along the forest paths to the largest building in the area—Arnold's home and the communal meeting place for the sleuth. A few werebears sat on the long couches and watched in apparent curiosity as Arnold led them inside the living room and over to a side door he quickly unlocked. They all followed him down the set of stairs behind it.

They were met with three barred doors at the bottom of the stairs, all three revealing empty cells. Arnold paused, staring at the leftmost door and the empty cell behind it.

"He was here. I promise you!" Arnold was gaping incredulously, clearly unable to understand what had happened.

Yani reached out and grabbed the door handle. He pulled, rattling the window bars as the door proved to be firmly locked. He stepped back to let everyone else have a chance to look at the door, since he didn't see anything more amiss than the missing werebear.

Brandon growled as he sniffed along the ground in front of the empty cell. He kept snorting, as if something was offending his nose. Khan stepped up next to Brandon and bent slightly at the waist as he delicately sniffed the air.

"Any scent has been removed," Khan said, sounding incredulous, "yet I am unable to find the spell that caused it."

"I'm the only one with a key," Arnold added.

"There was magic used," Aaron said. He was standing with his hand over the lock on the door, frowning to himself as he studied whatever his own magic could tell him. Yani didn't see anything out of the ordinary, which was especially odd when magic was involved.

"If someone knew about my eyes, could they hide their magic from me?" Yani asked. He tried squinting at the lock when Aaron removed his hand but still couldn't see anything.

"It would take a considerable amount of power," Khan replied. "I could accomplish such a feat with a week of preparation, but I would be utterly exhausted afterward. The person who has been concocting the dark spells I have been eating could do such a thing."

One name immediately jumped to the forefront of Yani's mind. The uneasy glances he shared with the others told him they were thinking the same thing.

"Cain could do it," Yani murmured.

"Who is Cain?" Khan asked curiously.

Aaron answered. He had spent the most time trying to find a way to stop Cain when they were finally able to locate him again.

"We're not entirely certain who or what Cain is. We believe he or she is an unseelie sidhe, but no one's been able to confirm that. Cain captured all of us a few years ago with the help of an ifrit djinni, and while we were able to escape by destroying the djinni, we haven't been able to find Cain since."

"You defeated an ifrit? Quite impressive." Khan sounded honestly impressed. "It would certainly be interesting to see if I could aid in your search. I will come along with you to the coalition headquarters, at least until the ursa traitor has been located."

"At the very least we can give every bear's house a sniff and see if we can get a name and face to match the scent from Khan's mountain and Maki's room." Luke looked resolute, but Yani didn't miss the desperate look he shot Brandon after he finished speaking. Brandon was stuck in wolf form until they figured out the spell that had trapped him, which had to be torture for Luke. As an incubus, Luke fed on sex. Yani might have been feeling deprived, thanks to Aaron's separation, but Luke needed sex to live. Within a few days, he would start getting ill.

"We need to figure out the spell on Brandon and Maki first thing," Yani added, to ensure everyone was on the same page.

"Agreed," Aaron said with his own contemplative glance at Brandon.

"It is merely a matter of willpower," Khan said dismissively. "If he has the incentive, the wolf will turn back on his own. I am much more interested in searching for the missing bear."

Aaron scowled at Khan but kept his mouth shut. Brandon looked as resolute as a wolf could, although he still hadn't changed shape, so just willpower alone clearly wasn't incentive enough to break the spell.

They all climbed back upstairs and followed Arnold as he led them from house to house throughout the woods. They started at John's home, and both Brandon and Khan were quick to agree that his scent didn't match.

It did match at Randy's house.

Yani remembered Randy snarling at Khan and being the most vocal advocate for Maki's execution. Now they knew why. Randy had been the one to plant the spell in Khan's forest and in Maki's bedside drawer. They didn't have a scent for whoever had planted the spell in the clearing, but it was a safe assumption at this point.

Arnold procured a key to the front door and let them into Randy's house. Aaron walked inside first and froze in place with a loud swear. Yani peeked over Aaron's shoulder and had to swallow back bile.

Randy was dead. Very, very dead. Someone had sliced open his stomach, reached into his body, and spread his organs and intestines across the floor. Blood was splashed liberally around the room, staining the carpet and the walls. Entrails and other body parts dotted the scene like grotesque monuments.

Yani stumbled back, still swallowing hard to keep from throwing up. That had to be the absolute worst thing he had ever seen.

"That looks like voodoo," Aaron murmured. "Like someone was trying to read a fortune with Randy's intestines."

"It's far older than mere voodoo, I'm afraid." Khan disagreed, which had Aaron frowning at him again.

"Voodoo has been around for generations," Aaron explained. "Usually they use a chicken for their black magic, but a human or were would work too."

"You said you were searching for an unseelie sidhe," Khan replied firmly. "Who do you think taught the darkest of death magic to humans in the first place?"

"You're saying this could be Cain's handiwork?" Luke asked.

"It is a distinct possibility," Khan replied with a nonchalant shrug. "Your enemy is certainly proving to be an interesting creature."

*

"I have been informed that the mage is currently in the Adirondacks looking into what caused you to go crazy and then become stuck in your panda form," Antoinette said as she stepped into view of the bars that were keeping Maki contained in her jail cell. "They're apparently hoping that if they can find the spell, they can also find a way to unravel it. When the mage returns, he'll have a look at you."

Antoinette had let the coalition know she was furious that the mage had chosen to go to the Adirondacks first before looking at Maki. All she got in return were platitudes, but then, that was all those werewolf fools could really offer. They didn't know how to break Maki free from her were-cage.

Maki nodded miserably and curled up into a tighter ball on the large bed in the back of the cell. She was depressed, Antoinette knew, and every day she couldn't change back weighed her down. If faced with the same situation, combined with the fact that Maki might have a death sentence hanging over her head, Antoinette would also sink to her lowest.

In fact, Antoinette had been almost exactly where Maki was early in her life.

"I was once stuck in a cage while trapped by my own personal chains," Antoinette said softly. Her private story of childhood hell wasn't something she shared easily, but Maki needed to know there was still hope. "I was still bleeding from the twenty lashes they had given me just before they led me to a cage. My master had tried to touch me, and I hit him for it, so they beat me and sold me to a chain gang working the docks. I was supposed to die, and I almost did. My wounds became infected, and I got very sick. They didn't feed me much, and I wasn't worth the medicine to heal. One day my shackles slipped off my wrists, I had grown so thin, and you know what I did? I put the damned things back on without anyone knowing they had ever come off and let them put me back in my cell for the night. Can you believe it?"

Maki was listening, at least. She could probably hear the waver in Antoinette's voice as incredulous tears at her stupidity colored her words, but she was listening. That was all Antoinette wanted.

"I lay there that night, wondering when I was going to die. It had to be soon if I was so emaciated the chains weren't staying on. I welcomed death because I knew it had to be far better than what my life was. I was so trapped in my own mind that it didn't occur to me that I had the means for escape. In fact, the idea didn't occur to me for almost a week. Another slave had found a rock and beaten his chains apart. He ran for it in broad daylight, the idiot, and was shot dead in the back. I had the thought that I could do the same and end my prolonged slide into death. That night, I took the too-large chains off my wrists and stared at the bars of my cell.

"The bars were mostly symbolic, you have to understand. I was chained to the wall, so my masters weren't worried that the bars were wide enough for someone as thin as I was to slide through easily. I took my chains off and stared at those bars and realized I didn't have to run into a firing squad. I had the cover of darkness, when my masters were asleep, and the element of surprise. Can you believe it didn't occur to me until that moment that death wasn't my only option? Looking back now, I can see how trapped I was within myself. I put my empty shackles down on the stiff pallet they had given me for a bed, slipped through the bars, snuck onto a ship, and I lived."

Maki had gotten off the bed and shuffled closer to Antoinette as Antoinette spoke. She solemnly held out one large paw through the bars, and Antoinette placed her own small hand into Maki's.

"There's more to the story after, and I'll tell it to you sometime, but escaping just that one desperate situation was easily the hardest thing I've ever done in my life, and I've been alive for a very long time, Maki," Antoinette whispered. She stared at her dark hand in Maki's white-furred paw, taking comfort from the contact. "Don't let yourself be trapped here. Choose to live, fight for your life. We'll get that mage down here to fix what's wrong, and you'll get out of here. I promise I won't let you die."

Maki used her free paw to wipe tears off her cheeks and nodded. They stayed together like that, hand in paw, until the rising sun forced Antoinette to bed for the day.

Chapter Two

Alone

The dorms in the Supernatural Coalition building were unchanged from the last time Yani had bunked there. Six twin beds filled the room, each with a small dresser at the foot for clothing and tchotchkes. It was supposed to be temporary housing for those in need, and Yani was just glad a bed was available for him.

Yani had packed up the essentials from the apartment while Aaron had finally gone to see Maki. It was cowardly to sneak off while Aaron was away, but Yani couldn't handle more of Aaron's bewildered looks or confused attempts to mend fences. Aaron understood that he had done something wrong. He knew it was his fault and he needed to fix it, but Yani was going to stick to Mom's advice and make a clean break.

If Aaron continued to work hard and kept from getting lost in his research again—basically if the man Yani had fallen in love with returned—Yani might reconsider his position. The last thing he wanted was to take Aaron back only to be forced to endure months of loneliness again.

Khan let out a heavy breath filled with disgust as he sank into the bed next to Yani's.

"My request for a single room was denied," Khan grumbled. "They are apparently set aside for medical emergencies and visiting alphas. In what world am I not an alpha?"

"Sorry, Khan," Yani replied with a shrug. There wasn't anything he could do to help.

"At least I have the pleasure of your company."

Yani couldn't stop a grin from growing at Khan's words, yet at the same time, he wanted to find an excuse to take a step back. Khan was definitely flirting with Yani, and Yani wasn't ready for any sort of relationship just yet. At least, he didn't think he was ready. His libido, on the other hand, saw a very handsome man and wanted to jump Khan and start licking all those beautiful black scales. It was Yani's bruised heart, his lingering and persistent feelings for Aaron, and the fact that his brain that kept yelling "bad idea!" at him that stopped him from following through with his fantasies.

Luckily, he had a real excuse to escape this time because he was pretty certain Khan knew exactly what was going through Yani's mind.

"I have a meeting with Alpha Karr. I'll see you later," Yani said bluntly, instead of answering Khan's flirtations. He stood from his bed, nodded politely to Khan, and headed out into the hallway.

It didn't take long to walk to Bishop's office. It was on the third floor of the building, only a few staircases and long hallways away from the dorms. It had a huge window that overlooked the surrounding forest, which was probably good for Bishop since he was a werewolf who no doubt preferred the woods to the tame office he was stuck in day after day. Yani knocked and stepped inside when he heard Bishop's okay through the wooden door.

The sun was shining through the window and over the trees. Yani couldn't help comparing the perpetually damp Adirondack forest to the one he could see spread out below and was glad yet again that he lived here.

Bishop Karr was an elderly man. His hair was white and his face cragged with wrinkles, but his smile was kind and his back straight with authority. He had been president of the coalition for as long as Yani had known the magical world existed and was also the alpha of the local werewolf pack. The responsibility only seemed to make Bishop stronger, and Yani really liked him.

"I've actually been meaning to speak with your entire team, but I'm happy to begin with you, Yani," Bishop said politely as Yani took one of the chairs across from Bishop's large wooden desk. "Your team has been amazingly successful, and I want to replicate that success. Before you told me about your issue with Aaron, I was going to ask to temporarily split your team in two for a few months. Brandon and Luke would train two people interested in learning the job, and you and Aaron would have done the same.

"I obviously can't pair you and Aaron together, and until Brandon recovers, I can't send them out either. Which means I need to come up with another plan."

"Sorry," Yani began, but Bishop waved him off.

"Life happens. I completely understand. I'm afraid that I'll need to put you on a desk job until I'm able to figure something out."

Yani nodded. At least he still had a job.

"I've read your report on the situation with the bears," Bishop continued. "I am aware that your prime suspect was eviscerated and that you have hit a dead end. I believe Aaron is attempting to break Maki's and Brandon's curses in order to learn whether Maki has any insight as to who attacked her. I have shown the necklace to Myobu Sensei, and she agreed with your assessment that it is a good-luck charm. I am going to recommend we find more comfortable accommodations for Maki in light of your findings."

That made sense to Yani, and he was glad to hear it.

"Let me know if there's anything I can do to help," he said.

"I appreciate that. We still want your team on the front lines against Cain, so my priority is getting all of you healthy again. That includes getting Aaron's head yanked back on straight," Bishop added wryly. "I was sad to hear how out of touch he has gotten, and I'll be having a lengthy conversation with him about it. I hope that in the future you can be work partners again."

Yani wasn't willing to say yes or no to that, at least not yet. The car ride home had cemented that fact clearly in his mind. Sitting behind Aaron, unable to think of anything to say to the man he had once loved above all others, had been incredibly awkward. Besides, a clean break meant he shouldn't be talking to Aaron at all anyway.

"Well," Bishop murmured when Yani didn't answer, "that's for the future. For now, we do actually need someone with your expertise in the administrative offices. Report to Julio at nine tomorrow morning. Oh, and if you see that dragon you brought back, ask him to please stop bothering the kelpie staying in our main lake house this weekend."

"I will. Thanks," Yani said. He stood and shook Bishop's hand before leaving the office. He stepped out into the hallway and paused, unsure about which direction to go. There wasn't anything on his schedule for the rest of the day. Maki's case had hit a dead end, so he couldn't work on anything there. Yani didn't really want to go back to the dorms where Khan was waiting. The potential for something untoward happening was a little too high, and Yani was honestly feeling a little too emotionally unstable to handle Khan's attentions at the moment.

The sad truth was, outside of his job and his little circle of friends, Yani didn't have much of a life. His hobbies had been usurped by training his vision, and his free time was usually spent at work. It was pretty damned depressing to know he had nothing to do and no one to hang out with. He felt like a schlub, which was ridiculous, but true. He needed to figure out how to get his own life back on track.

No ideas immediately came to mind. Yani sighed heavily and picked a random direction. The coalition building was huge, with plenty of rooms Yani hadn't seen yet. He might as well wander until a better idea appeared.

*

Julio was an ordinary-looking man. He had lightly tanned skin, light brown hair, and light brown eyes. Yani had never met someone so unmemorable before. He could literally walk past Julio anywhere inside the coalition building and not remember him.

"Alpha Karr told me to report to you today," Yani explained when Julio stared uncomprehendingly at Yani for a few long moments.

"Ah, yes." Julio nodded.

Julio's voice was low and heavily accented. It wasn't Spanish, but Yani didn't know enough about European languages to figure out which language was coloring Julio's vowels.

"Alpha Karr dropped this on me last minute, you understand, so while I know your background, I don't have anything ready for you just yet. For the moment, we're going to start you off with filing. It's a job that needs to be done, and while you're busy with that, I'll start arranging a real position for you." Julio smiled at Yani kindly, no doubt completely understanding that the last thing Yani wanted to be doing was filing. Still, this was a job that would allow him to keep his steady paycheck with benefits, so Yani couldn't complain. "If you walk to the end of the room that way," Julio continued, pointing off to Yani's right, "there's a locked door. Put your finger on the scanner, and you'll be allowed in. Your prints are already in the system. Everything is labeled; it just needs to be organized. Keep everything you read confidential, and we won't have a problem."

That was clearly a dismissal. Yani nodded to Julio before turning and walking through the room to his right.

The administrative offices were on the first floor of the building, near the front entrance. When Yani had first been introduced to the world of magic, his visits to the coalition had been strictly controlled. He had only been allowed to see one of the three small sitting rooms by the main entrance and the equally small kitchen that provided tea and snacks to the temporary visitors who used those rooms. There was a long hallway off the kitchen that led to the rest of the building and the first room off that hallway was the administrative offices. Julio's desk was at the very front of the room, and at least a hundred other desks filled the space in even rows behind and to either side of Julio's.

Yani walked carefully behind chairs filled with all sorts of creatures, humanoid and not. Most of them sparkled slightly in his sight, and he had to look carefully to make certain he didn't step on a tentacle that was real versus the various intangible limbs he also saw.

The doorway Julio had sent him to was easy enough to find—the only one along the otherwise empty wall. Yani didn't see a handle, but a fingerprint scanner was recessed into the wall. Yani didn't know which finger he was supposed to use, so he chose one at random. His right pointer finger apparently worked, because the machine beeped softly, and the door popped open. He stepped through, and the door shut automatically behind him.

The room he entered was easily as big as the giant one he had just left behind. Six ten-foot tables were evenly spaced through the center of the room, and all six were completely covered in piles of file folders. The perimeter of the room was entirely filled with colored filing cabinets. The colors were grouped together and coordinated with a large sign on the wall overhead. Red was Massachusetts, green was Vermont, yellow was New Hampshire, purple was Maine, white was Connecticut, brown was Rhode Island, and the smallest bank of cabinets were blue for Albany, New York. The individual cabinets were then labeled ongoing, completed, and cold.

Yani walked over to the nearest table and picked up the top folder. The label area had a red sticker on it that read Springfield, MA. At least Yani could tell where the folder belonged, although he didn't see any indication whether it was ongoing, completed, or cold. He flipped open the folder and skimmed through the top page.

The folder was barely a week old, according to what he read. A king cobra shifter had been found dead in a back alley. The local police were handling it as a general murder investigation. They no doubt thought the shifter was human, but since this was the first time Yani had ever heard of a king cobra shifter, that wasn't too surprising. He couldn't imagine what a king cobra was even doing in Massachusetts. Didn't they live in warmer climates? The case was definitely still ongoing.

Yani walked over to the red filing cabinets and pulled open one of the drawers labeled as ongoing. He luckily found the Springfield section quickly and slotted the folder into place. Then he turned back to the six long tables filled with similar folders and let out a heavy sigh.

This sucked. It was no wonder the room had gotten so messy, considering how thankless a job this was going to be. Only Yani had been stupid enough to volunteer to take any position available in the coalition in order to keep his job. At least this was only supposed to be temporary.

Well, Yani might have been shuffled into a shitty job, but at least he was still employed. He was actually a little worried that if Aaron didn't get his head on straight soon he would lose his job, but then, it wasn't really Yani's problem any longer now that they had broken up.

He chose one table at random and pulled a stack of folders toward him. Each one was at least color coded. Yani picked up the stack and started walking in circles around the room, carefully placing each folder on the floor in front of the corresponding bank of cabinets. Though he was going to make a mess, at least it would be a better organized mess. Once he had a few of the tables cleared, he could start using them instead of the floor for each state, and then he could start going through the folders to figure out where they should actually be filed.

He was bored just thinking about it, but he had a plan and a whole hour of freedom for lunch to look forward to.

*

Yani's brain was beyond numb by the time he finally escaped. Julio was gone from his desk already, so Yani didn't bother hanging around. He took the closest staircase up to the floor the dorms were on and then headed through the long hallways to reach that part of the building.

"I do not enjoy being bored," Khan whined the second Yani stepped into the room. Khan was draped over his bed like a lizard on a warm rock in the sun. "I left my library back in my cave, and everyone is far too busy to entertain me. This is unacceptable, Yani."

Yani was too mentally brain-dead to deal with this. He flopped down on his own bed with a groan and rubbed his eyes with one hand. He ought to be feeling accomplished since he had managed to completely unearth all six tables. In the morning, he could get the stacks of files off the floor and start putting them away. Instead, he just felt sad and lonely.

His job used to be fun. Even when they were investigating something gruesome, he had always had Aaron to lean on and Brandon and Luke to joke with. It wasn't just the constant mass of folders that was the problem, if he was being honest with himself. The filing room had been silent except for the noise he had made. With no one to talk to, Yani had started muttering to himself, which only highlighted how alone he really was.

Mom had insisted a clean break would solve his relationship issues, but in some ways, Yani was starting to think fondly back to the days where he had been sitting in silence next to an engrossed Aaron. At least then he'd had the sounds of Aaron's breathing and page turning. Plus, just having Aaron nearby had provided some comfort in knowing that he might have felt alone, but he wasn't really. Down in that filing room, Yani had zero doubts that he was utterly and completely alone.

"None of that, now," Khan said, interrupting Yani's scattered thoughts. Sharp-nailed fingers brushed along Yani's cheeks, wiping away tears Yani didn't even realize he was shedding. "Come. It is the time you humans customarily eat, is it not? I shall accompany you to the dining hall. We will have pleasant conversation, and then you might tell me what is ailing you."

Yani nodded, looking into Khan's dark eyes, which were very concerned. "I—" His voice cracked, and Yani had to swallow hard before he tried again. "I think I'd like that."

"Good. Then go wash your face and let's be off."

Yani obeyed. The communal bathroom was thankfully empty as he stumbled inside. There weren't many visitors at the moment needing beds, so he wasn't disturbed as he washed his face to clear away the evidence that he had been crying.

The mirror reflected how wan and almost sick he looked. Maybe it was the lighting, but his skin looked yellowish. His brown hair, usually so curly, was limp. He had showered that morning, so he couldn't understand why he looked as bad as he did. He could be getting sick. All the stress of the last few months—and the last few days in particular—was probably catching up with him.

Yani braced his hands on the counter and let out a heavy breath.

"This is just temporary," he told his reflection. It was just the aftermath of his breakup and the interim job. He could get through this, and everything would be better on the other side. It had to be.

Yani's reflection looked skeptical, so Yani turned away with a huff to go find Khan and head to dinner.

The dining hall wasn't full, but there were enough people there that the chatter drowned out Yani's negative thoughts. He filled a plate from the buffet and followed Khan to two empty seats. Yani ate in silence for a few moments, forcing the food down even though it made him feel slightly nauseous. When he had enough, he turned to Khan.

"Tell me something about dragons," Yani said.

Khan swallowed his bite of steak—lightly seared on the outside and still rare on the inside—before answering.

"What do you want to know?" Khan said with a smile. "Dragons aren't exactly common. I doubt you will run into another in your lifetime."

"But I've met you," Yani insisted, "and I would like to know more about you."

"Ah," Khan breathed, looking pleased. "I am happy to tell you about myself. Dragons are pure magic. We coalesce that magic into a form, be it dragon, snake, or human-shaped. Some dragons prefer to be garden snakes, happy to live their lives in simplicity. It's a pleasant existence, albeit a boring one. I much prefer to have a presence. For people to notice me and be awed." He sounded just as arrogant as his words implied, but Yani could see the way his eyes were shining and knew Khan was describing what made him happy. "Since we are magic, we can use it fairly easily. Of course, if I use too much, I might lose my form until I am able to gather enough magic to coalesce again. It is a delicate balance. Tell me about your eyes-that-see."

Yani looked down at his half-eaten dinner for a moment, unsure whether to be pleased Khan was asking about him or embarrassed because his story certainly wasn't as remarkable as Khan's. Still, Khan did seem interested.

"I honestly didn't know anything about them until two years ago," Yani explained. "We were fighting an ifrit djinni, and I saw through the glamour it was using to hide itself. Luke also forced me into the dream plane to escape it, and all I saw were endless clouds instead of the dreamscape. Aaron tested how strong my eyes were with some illusions, and I could see through even his strongest. Then Cain grabbed us, and he painted a spell in blood on my skin to enhance my sight. He wanted to steal it for himself when he killed me, but we somehow managed to escape first. I've been able to see through illusions and identify spells ever since."

"It's something that only manifests in family lines that are touched by vampirism," Khan said leadingly.

Yani nodded. "To escape the Nazis, my grandmother and her family ended up hiding in a vampire's house. Uncle Martin took them in and kept them safe, and Uncle Yakov, my grandmother's younger brother, fell in love with Uncle Martin. They've been together ever since."

Khan nodded thoughtfully. "Even if your Uncle Martin never touched anyone aside from Yakov, his presence would still have imbued your family with some sort of strength, especially if he was a very old vampire. It is a common effect for those who live around magic, and for some reason, vampirism allows for extraordinary senses to develop. I suspect your entire family has lived long and healthy lives."

No one really knew Gramma Chana's age when she died, since her birth certificate had been lost, but she had been over one hundred. None of Gramma's children had ever gotten seriously sick, and they were all alive and well, if suffering from the effects of old age. Grandpa Gideon was almost as old as Gramma when she had passed, and he still went for a walk outside every day. Yani had never really gotten sick either. He had the usual colds in the winter, but when everyone at school got chicken pox or the flu, he had stayed healthy.

Uncle Martin was an extremely old vampire. Yani had never asked how old, but he was powerful enough to subdue an entire coven of rampaging vampires without any issues. Bishop had been impressed with Martin, Yani remembered that.

"I guess that's where my powers come from," Yani said finally, after a long moment of silence. "I never knew that before."

"It isn't common knowledge," Khan replied with an offhand shrug. "It used to be, but magic has changed over the last few hundred years, and it was forgotten and replaced with new information. Although, the magic your mage used was quite ancient."

Yani managed not to wince at the mention of Aaron and answered anyway. "It's Kabbalism, ancient Jewish magic created at least five thousand years ago."

"He was quite strong," Khan admitted, "although something wasn't quite right with him. I can't put my finger on what it was, but I feel like I should recognize it. I would like to have another look at him while he performs a spell. Do you know where he might be?"

"Probably stuck in a stupid book somewhere," Yani grumbled scathingly.

Khan blinked in surprise, and then his face softened. "Forgive me, Yani. I have forgotten to be considerate of your recent pain. Let us speak of something else for a time, so you might go to sleep with a happy conversation in mind."

They both got dessert, and then Khan made certain to keep the conversation light and easy. They talked about Yani's childhood and his family, about the new baby on his father's side, and about some of Khan's funnier exploits throughout the years. Yani went to bed that night smiling. Khan was in another bed next to him, still grumbling about the poor accommodations, when Yani fell asleep.

He didn't feel any better in the morning, but he also didn't feel any worse. He grabbed a quick breakfast with Khan before heading back to the administration offices. Yani hesitated for a long moment with his finger over the scanner, trying to get himself ready for another long and boring day. He took a deep breath to brace himself before finally putting his finger onto the scanner and walking into the room when the door obligingly popped open.

All of his sorted folders were still on the floor in front of their respective filing cabinets. A new, thankfully small, stack of folders was on one of the cleared tables. Yani picked up that stack first and quickly sorted the folders into the right piles before he turned toward the largest pile.

Massachusetts was apparently a hotbed for supernatural activity, as it had the most files. He stacked all the files onto the nearest table and with a heavy sigh, opened the topmost one. He had to read through until he found where it said whether the case was still ongoing, closed, or cold, and then put the folder in the correct filing cabinet. There needed to be a spot at the top of the paperwork where that information could be written so it could then be filed quickly. Instead, Yani would have to read every single one of the hundreds of folders in order to get them put away correctly.

It was going to be an unbelievably tedious day.

There were reports on just about everything. Petty larceny, minor disputes, major disputes, murders. Anything that was considered illegal that had been committed by a supernatural creature had been researched and placed into a folder. It didn't matter if the local human police had handled it—unknowing of the supernatural element, of course—or whether the coalition had needed to step in. A file had been created regardless.

"Murdered albino werewolf. Ongoing," Yani muttered to himself as he filed that folder under Nantucket. He didn't even bother to wonder what a werewolf was doing living there. It wasn't any stranger than Jangjamari living in Plymouth. A Korean water spirit shouldn't have been able to survive in the cold waters of the northern Atlantic, yet she had been living a perfectly healthy life before someone had cut her throat. Most of the folders were nonviolent in nature: fights that had broken out and been solved, simple misunderstandings between a landlord and a mermaid that had fallen asleep in her bathtub and accidentally flooded the apartment below hers. Yani had half of the Massachusetts pile filed before lunch and was able to get it all completed before quitting time.

His fingers ached from flipping through paper. He had a few paper cuts that were more annoying than anything. Yani also had the beginning of a stress headache from reading all the small, cramped print all day. He felt exhausted and slightly ill. Acid was churning in his stomach, and he thought he might be running a low-grade fever.

Khan met him at the doorway to the dorms, took one look at Yani, and scowled. "Soup tonight, I think. Go take a hot shower, and I'll bring you something easy to swallow." He pulled Yani into a hug, and Yani couldn't help sinking into the warmth of Khan's body and the strength in Khan's arms. It was the best thing he had felt all day.

It must have something to do with being a dragon, but Khan's body was unnaturally warm and that heat seeped into Yani's bones, warming him from the inside. Some of his aches faded away just because he finally felt like he could take a deep breath. His shoulders relaxed, which erased some of the tension in his head and back.

Khan pulled away slightly so he could look at Yani. One of his hands settled onto Yani's cheek, and he gently tilted Yani's face upward so he could look Yani in the eyes.

"Better?" Khan asked, his voice low and gentle. Yani nodded, feeling the scales on Khan's hand rub against his cheek. They were soft and supple, like snakeskin, rather than the hardened armor as most stories about dragons described them. Yani put his own hand on top of Khan's so he could feel the scales there, and Khan's eyes softened slightly as he looked at Yani. "You are a treasure, as beautiful as the brightest diamond, one I wish I could place in my caves and keep safe until the end of time. Yet you do not fear me as most humans do."

Khan's head tilted slightly, and for a moment, Yani thought Khan might bend down for a kiss. Yani would have reciprocated, but even as he was tilting his own head in invitation, Khan was pulling away. "I should get you that soup," he murmured, but Yani knew he was only being polite. Yani was only a week out of a bad breakup and was still feeling pretty torn up by it, but Khan was here in a way that Aaron hadn't been in a very long time.

Mom would be upset that Yani was interested in dating another goy. She wanted Yani to settle down with a nice Jewish boy—like Aaron—and start having kids. Khan was everything Mom didn't want for Yani, but that was just one more thing on the unfortunately long list of why Yani shouldn't be doing this right now. Yet he really didn't care about any of that. Khan was beautiful, and he wanted Yani just as much as Yani wanted him. A relationship required a starting point before it could grow and eventually address all the various issues Yani was ignoring, and Yani thought he knew exactly how to begin.

Yani reached out and gently grabbed Khan's shoulder to stop him from walking away before pushing up onto his tiptoes so he could reach Khan's mouth and take a chaste kiss.

Khan let out a low hiss, and his arms wrapped around Yani again. Their mouths pressed together, soft skin against even softer scales. Yani didn't know who opened first, but it was decidedly strange to be kissing someone with a forked tongue. It was thicker at the base and the two sides reached more of Yani's mouth than he was used to, but it wasn't a bad feeling at all. Yani was slowly getting hard, and he pushed his body close to Khan's in order to feel the friction as they stood together. Khan's own length pressed against Yani's stomach, and he rumbled in pleasure as Yani shifted.

The hug had been nice, but this was what Yani really needed. To feel loved, wanted, was better than anything in the world. It had been so damned long since anyone had even wanted to hold his hand, let alone kiss him, and Khan wanted to do all that and more.

"To the bed?" Khan hissed out in the brief moment their lips parted so they could breathe. Yani's wordless moan of assent was apparently enough as Khan bent down to resume their kiss. They shuffled together toward the nearest bed, not wanting to lose any contact, even for the brief moment it would take to walk the ten-foot distance.

The back of Yani's knees hit the side of the bed, and he let out a low groan. He wanted this, needed this so badly, but he also needed to get some of his clothing off before they fell into the mattress and it became much more difficult to get naked.

"I need to speak with you, now!" a woman's voice snarled as the door slammed open. Yani jumped in surprise and fell onto the bed. Khan let out a low growl and turned to snarl at the woman. She had dark skin and thick wavy hair. Her cheekbones were high, and overall, she was an absolutely beautiful woman. It took Yani a few seconds to recognize her: Antoinette, the leader of the local vampire coven.

"It can wait," Khan growled.

"No, it can't," Antoinette snarled back with her fangs flashing into view.

"And why not?" Khan replied, still growling. "You have interrupted us. Why would we want to help you now?"

"Not you," Antoinette said sharply as she pointed at Yani. "Him. I will speak with him at once."

Yani wasn't in a position to gainsay the vampire leader, no matter how compromising a position he had been found in.

"What do you need me for?" he asked.

"You need to tell that idiot mage to get back here! Alpha Karr insisted that as soon as the mage returned to town from the Adirondacks he would see to Maki, but he spent barely five minutes just looking at her before leaving. Now I hear he has left town again to Worcester to visit his family, but Maki is still suffering!"

Aaron's mother lived in Worcester. She was the one teaching him Kabbalism, and Yani didn't doubt he had gone to her for help on what was wrong with his magic. He didn't want to tell Antoinette that, though, and give her the impression that Aaron wasn't as strong as she had been told, which would paint Bishop as a liar.

"I think he went there to do some research," Yani explained, which was also true. "His magic teacher lives in Worcester, and he probably needed her advice on how to break the spell. Our friend Brandon was cursed too." And Yani hadn't taken a few minutes to call Luke and see how they were doing, he remembered with a pang of shame. What kind of friend was he? Not a good one, obviously.

"He had better be back soon. Maki won't be able to handle it much longer," Antoinette said loftily. "Sorry for interrupting," she added with a sheepish smile as she headed back out the door. She closed it behind her, leaving Yani and Khan alone again.

The mood was gone. Khan sneered at the door before collapsing onto his bed across from Yani.

"I haven't called Luke or Brandon in two days," Yani whispered. He was looking at his hands, watching them shake slightly. He was feeling sick again, his stomach rolling as much as his mind.

"Call them and shower. I'll bring you some soup and see about getting you some medicine," Khan said softly. "We can talk later."

Yani nodded and reached for his phone. He didn't have any missed calls or texts, which assuaged some of the guilt. They would have called him if something had happened. Khan left the room as Yani typed in Luke's number and hit Call.

"Hey, Yani," Luke answered on the third ring. He sounded as bad as Yani felt, his voice scratchy and tight.

"Hey, Luke. How are you and Brandon holding up?"

Luke sighed heavily. "Brandon is spending every moment trying to figure out how to shift forms. I'm having to conserve as much energy as I can, but I'm not going to last another week without having to do something drastic. Anyway, what have you been up to?"

"Bishop sent me to the administrative offices, where they have me filing." Yani let out a sigh at the reminder. "It's awful. I miss you guys."

"We've all been together for so long, it's hard to suddenly be split up. Brandon and I understand, but it's tough to try to get healthy without everyone here to help like usual. Hopefully Aaron will figure out what's wrong with Brandon and Maki with his mother's help. I don't want to talk about it right now. Is anything else happening at the coalition other than your taking over their filing?"

"I made out with Khan," Yani admitted.

"You did?" That brought back the Luke that Yani remembered. His voice lost the tired edge and was replaced by his usual sly lasciviousness. "Tell me more!"

"He's been flirting with me since we got back, and things escalated tonight." Yani licked his lips at the memory. "Have you ever kissed someone with a forked tongue before?"

Luke let out a shout of laughter. "Best blow job ever, let me tell you." There was a pointed *woof* in the background, and Luke's voice came through the speaker from a distance. "You do a great job, love, don't worry. Your tongue just can't go in two directions at the same time. It's hard for anyone to compete." His voice came back to the speaker as he spoke to Yani again. "Go for it, Yani. Enjoy yourself and I'll live vicariously through you."

Yani laughed. "As if you haven't done it all dozens of times before."

"True, but I'm not into bestiality, so all I'm getting right now is through your stories. I think this is my longest drought since before I hit puberty." His voice was starting to sound scratchy again, as if the reminder had erased all of his lust-induced humor. "Anyway, I should go. Someone is starting to get mats in his fur, and I promised to give him a good brushing."

"All right. I'll see you soon, I hope?"

"We'll make sure of it. I think Brandon wants to move into the werewolf house and see if they'll be able to help him shift, so we'll be right next door tomorrow. We'll come visit."

"Looking forward to it," Yani replied. They said goodbye and then Yani hung up.

Brandon hadn't figured out how to break the curse yet, but he wasn't getting any worse or losing spirit like Maki. That was good to know. It was Luke that Yani was worried about. If Luke didn't have sex soon, he would start fading away into the dream world and wouldn't have the strength to return, but Brandon was his mate, which meant that only he could help Luke now. They were running out of time, and Yani was sitting impotently on his bed, unable to do anything about it.

Yani coughed weakly and levered himself to his feet. His chest was tight with worry, and whatever sickness he was coming down with only made it worse. There had to be a book in the library that would help, something he could research that would get Brandon back to his human form. Yet Aaron had read just about every magic book he could get his hands on, including the ones in the vast coalition library. Yani had no doubt at all that the first thing Aaron had done when they had gotten back from Bolton Landing was head to the library. It would be foolishly redundant for Yani to waste his time crawling in Aaron's footsteps. He let out a heavy breath and gathered his shower things instead. Khan had said to get in a warm shower, and maybe while Yani was doing that, a better idea of how to help would come to him.

*

The shower did feel nice. His headache and the pain between his shoulder blades lessened in the heat. Khan was waiting when Yani walked back into the dorm room. There was a tray on Yani's bedside table with a bowl of steaming soup and two crusty rolls.

"Eat," Khan insisted. He was watching Yani hungrily, his eyes on Yani's bare chest still slightly damp from the shower and on the waistband of his low-slung boxer shorts. He didn't allow his interest to distract him, though. Yani looked back at Khan, knowing his own interest was plain on his face. "Eat," Khan reiterated. "We need to actually talk before we resume any carnal relations. It is still too soon since your breakup for us to be serious, but I want to be. We will have to take it slow."

"Slow," Yani agreed, "but not too slow." He wasn't feeling bad about Aaron any longer. There was still a pang in his heart for what they had once had, but he couldn't seem to make himself remember to care that it had only been days since his breakup. He did remember being pretty torn up at the time, yet he wasn't upset at all now. His interest in Khan was much more prominent.

Yani sat down on his bed and obediently picked up the bowl of soup. Maybe once he'd eaten, Khan would be willing to pick up where they'd left off before Antoinette had interrupted. The soup was hearty, full of bits of chicken and potato and thick with chopped vegetables. It took a few bites before Yani's stomach decided whether he was starving or too nauseous to eat, but hunger won. He finished the entire bowl and both rolls within minutes.

The bowl clanked as Yani put it back on the tray, and he let out a wide yawn. He blinked, but the bowl wouldn't come into focus. Yani slowly turned to look at Khan, and the world gently spun around him as sleep insistently beckoned.

"Go to sleep, Yani," Khan said with a gentle smile on his face.

"You drugged me?" Yani tried to ask. It came out more slur than words, but Khan understood.

"You're sick and need a good night's sleep. I simply ensured that you would be uninterrupted tonight."

Yani's body slumped downward, unable to remain sitting upright any longer. Khan gently caught him and helped him beneath the covers. As Yani's eyes slid closed, he felt the press of Khan's lips against his forehead and a wash of pleasant tingling erupted from that site and spread through his body. Sleep came moments later, pulling Yani away before he could ask Khan what magic spell he had just used.

*

"I am going to kill him," Antoinette hissed under her breath. "I'll drink all of his blood, and I won't feel guilty about it. At all. How dare he leave town on vacation when someone needs his help!" She turned the last corner of the basement hallway and stepped into view of the cell door.

Two men immediately turned to look at her in surprise. One was holding the key to the cell door; the other had a gun strapped to his hip.

"What is going on here?" she snapped, only noticing that Maki wasn't crying after she spoke.

"Our investigators have proven her innocence," the man with the key explained. "We are going to show her to more pleasant quarters that will suffice until she is able to shift back to a human."

Antoinette couldn't help smiling at the admission that Maki was innocent, which she had known all along, but that smile faded quickly.

"What are you going to do, put her out in the barn with the kelpies? I think not. Maki, would you like to stay with me? It will be a bit tight for a large panda, but more comfortable than the barn."

Maki's eyes widened in surprise, but she nodded. It was hard to tell in a panda's face, but Antoinette thought Maki might be smiling. Antoinette had to smile back.

"She's free to do what she wants as a visitor to the coalition," the man replied with a shrug. "We have comfortable accommodations available for her, but it doesn't matter to me where she stays."

He unlocked the cell door and pulled it open wide. Maki hurried out into the hallway as if she couldn't stay behind bars for another moment more, but she paused to bow politely to the men in thanks before turning toward Antoinette.

Antoinette reached out and was gratified when Maki sat on her haunches and reached out one large paw as well. Small, dark fingers touched the softness of the white-and-black fur on the back of her paw, but they couldn't hold hands with Maki in panda form, so Antoinette dropped her arm back to her side and Maki stood to resume walking.

"Let me show you where you can stay. We can take the connecting tunnel," Antoinette explained. She turned back the way she had come, and Maki fell into step next to her. The rest of the walk back to the vampire building was quiet. Maki looked around at everything they walked past and breathed deeply of the air of freedom. It had taken Antoinette weeks of scrabbling through dirty London streets after her endless time on the ship before she realized that she had truly escaped the chains that had held her.

Standing and breathing air that was as free and clear as she was became one of the better moments of her life, so she encouraged Maki to do so as well.

The majority of the vampire house was underground by necessity. Only two floors were visible from the outside, mostly for show or for the few human visitors. The tunnel let out on the second basement level, and Antoinette immediately led Maki upstairs, where windows would let in fresh air and bright sunlight during the day, something she was certain Maki was missing.

The previous coven leader had kept two rooms, one in the basement and one on the top floor. He used them, depending on who and when he had visitors, and had lavishly appointed both. A king-sized bed, large chairs, and a bathroom with a soaker tub large enough to fit a bear were only a few of the amenities. Every handle, from the doors to the faucets, were levers sturdy enough for vampire strength or animal paws. Antoinette wanted Maki to be comfortable.

"This room is yours for as long as you want it," Antoinette explained. "You'll have to go over to the coalition building for food. I'm certain they'll be able to accommodate you." Antoinette pulled the curtains open on one of the large windows so Maki could see the bright lights of the coalition building through the thick trees that surrounded both houses. The sun was barely down for the night and dinner preparations were underway, so the dining hall was brilliantly lit. "During the day, there are six vampires sleeping in the basement. I would appreciate it if you would leave them be. I will speak with them all tonight so they know you have this room and won't bother you either."

Maki looked around the room with wide eyes, taking in the space eagerly. Then she glanced down at her oversized paws and let out a heavy, depressed sigh.

The fury that Antoinette had suppressed when she realized Maki had been found innocent redoubled, blazing in her heart. She would find that mage and wring his neck for leaving Maki in this state.

"Don't worry. This is a vampire house. We're considerably stronger than humans, so the entire building has been specially reinforced. Everything in this room should be able to handle the weight and strength of a panda. You can sleep in a real bed and wash in the tub without worry."

Maki turned to Antoinette. Her eyes were soft with gratitude as she bowed low in thanks. Maki held the bow for a few long seconds, far longer than really necessary to emphasize how much she appreciated what Antoinette was doing for her.

"If you need anything at all, just ask," Antoinette insisted. She held out her hands when Maki finished her bow, and Maki sat back and put her paws gently into Antoinette's. "We'll figure this out, together. Just stay strong." She squeezed Maki's paws gently. "Now, go take a bath and get the stench of prison off your fur, and I'll see about having dinner brought over for you."

Maki nodded in agreement and she was definitely smiling.

Antoinette left her to it and headed outside. Now that the sun was fully down, she could take the quicker aboveground route. She stopped in one of the larger kitchens first to get someone started on packing a dinner for Maki, then headed deeper into the building.

The mage had gone on vacation, so Maki couldn't pummel him yet. Alpha Karr had proven to be entirely unhelpful, so she would need to go around him for this matter. She did know that there was a werewolf and incubus that worked with the mage, but they lived off-site. There was a human affiliated with the mage that the rumor mill said had recently moved into the dorms. She would talk with him.

It wasn't too hard to find the dorms, and only one of the rooms had occupants inside. She burst in, already yelling her complaints, and was stopped short by the scene inside. The human was kissing a creature that was most decidedly not human. Not just kissing, either.

Antoinette was lucky she hadn't been a few minutes later because she was certain she would have interrupted something much more intimate. Still, she couldn't be sorry. Learning that the mage hadn't actually gone on vacation, but was instead visiting his mentor for help figuring out the spell on Maki was a relief. Maybe she wouldn't kill him after all.

She left them to their activities and went to procure the food she had ordered for Maki.

Hopefully it wouldn't be too much longer before she could hold Maki's hands in her own. The paws were cute, but Antoinette wanted to see the face behind the fur and to know if the person she was quickly falling for was as beautiful as her lovely spirit implied.

Chapter Three

Darkness

Yani's next two days were more of the same. Khan was making himself scarce, which didn't help alleviate the doldrums. Obviously, Khan wasn't nearly as interested in Yani as he was in Khan.

Yani went to work during the day and then choked down dinner every night. Since he hadn't thrown up yet, he felt it was safe to assume the constant nausea was caused by something other than a stomach bug. He wasn't eating much, though. After dinner, he took a bath and went to bed. The only times he saw Khan at all were when he tossed himself awake at night and saw Khan sleeping in the next bed.

The days of filing were starting to take their toll. His whole body ached from all the bending over he was doing to get the files sorted properly. He had finished with Rhode Island and New Hampshire and was ready to start with Maine in the morning, but he desperately didn't want to. What he wanted was to crawl into bed and stay there indefinitely.

Yani was just finishing dinner on the third night when his phone rang. He almost didn't hear it over the din of the dining hall, but he hurried to deposit his dirty dishes in the return bin and get outside the room where he could hear.

Uncle Yakov had never called him back, which was odd, but Luke's number was on the screen when Yani looked.

"Is everything okay?" Yani asked.

"Maybe?" Luke replied. "I just got a call from Aaron. He's back and wants to meet with us in an hour. He's reserved one of the magic rooms in the coalition building. Will you be there?"

"Yes," Yani replied immediately. He hadn't had a chance to see his friends in days. He wanted to go, even it meant seeing Aaron too. Besides, Aaron was supposed to have gone to Worcester to consult with his mother. Aaron wouldn't be calling so soon after returning to Boston if he didn't have something. "We should probably tell Antoinette too."

"The vampire coven leader? Why?"

Yani laughed, realizing he hadn't told Luke about her awkward interruption the other day. "She's apparently become friends with Maki and stormed into my dorm room to inform me she was furious that Aaron had run off again without fixing Maki first."

"When was this?" Luke asked through his laughter. "Don't tell me—"

"Yep, Khan's tongue was down my throat and his hands were heading down my pants," Yani admitted.

"His forked tongue, you mean," Luke added with a sly giggle. "You try a blow job with him yet?"

"Not yet. He's been avoiding me, actually. Said we needed to talk before things progressed and then vanished." Yani sighed, wishing relationships could just be easy.

"Weird. Well, if you see him, bring him along. I want to have a look at his...tongue, and erm...evaluate him for you."

Yani let out a snort of laughter. "At his tongue, right. Just don't do anything that will make Brandon bite you. If I see Khan, I'll tell him."

"Tell me what?" Khan asked from behind Yani just as Yani hit the Disconnect button on his phone.

Yani jumped and spun around, then relaxed when he saw it was only Khan.

"Aaron's back from his mother's, and Luke thinks he may have found a solution. Luke wants me to bring you along," Yani explained. He started walking back to the dorm as he spoke. He needed to shower the day's aches away and get changed into something more comfortable before the meeting. There was still time if he hurried.

"You want me there in case Aaron is unable to control his magical abilities again?" Khan asked. His voice was light, so Yani knew he wasn't making fun of Aaron this time, just curious about Yani's intentions.

"Ah, no," Yani admitted. "Luke wants to interrogate you about our relationship."

"An incubus wishes to interrogate me?" Khan asked, sounding surprised. "How novel. I cannot even imagine the subject matter."

"Luke's an incubus. He hasn't just imagined the subject. He's probably performed all of it." Some of it had been with Yani for the few months they had been dating. "He's a good guy, though, so if he asks something you're uncomfortable with, just tell him and he'll back off."

"It should be quite interesting," Khan replied with a sly smile of his own that had Yani's brain flashing back to their long kiss from a few days ago. Khan's eyes gained a knowing twinkle as he grinned at Yani, but he shook his head. "Go shower and prepare for your meeting. I will go with you."

Yani sighed internally, but there wasn't enough time for anything fun. Maybe he could convince Khan to fool around after the meeting was over. Instead of pushing the subject, Yani went to find his towel and headed to the showers.

Forty-five minutes later, they were walking through the hallways again. The magic rooms were on the opposite side of the building from the living quarters, so it was a long walk to get there. Khan was content to walk in silence, so Yani didn't bother trying to talk to him yet. There would be time after the meeting, Yani had to remind himself. Now wasn't a good time.

They reached the practice room Aaron had reserved with a few minutes to spare, but they were the last ones there. Maki was sitting in a corner of the room, her huge body taking up most of the space. Antoinette was standing at her side, radiating anger in Aaron's direction.

Aaron was standing in the center of the room, next to the small table that was bolted in the center of every practice room. A rolled-up scroll was on the table just in front of him. He looked good, better than he had in months. His face had color and his eyes had life and, most tellingly, that damned book that hadn't left his side was nowhere to be found.

In contrast, Luke looked terrible. His cheeks were gaunt and his eyes sunken. He was sitting in one of the chairs, and Yani thought that was because he didn't have the strength to remain standing. Brandon was lying at Luke's feet, radiating protective worry from the stiffness in his shoulders to the way he curled defensively around Luke as if he could keep him safe just by being there.

Yani knew that he looked and felt somewhere between Aaron and Luke. He wasn't sickly looking, but he didn't look healthy either.

Aaron's face lit up when Yani walked into the room, but it fell when Khan immediately followed. Yani tried not to read too much into that. He wasn't about to jump back into Aaron's arms now that Aaron looked normal again. Yani had Khan to think about now.

"I'm going to try to explain everything," Aaron said once Yani had taken the other chair and settled in. "It's a lot to get out, so please don't interrupt."

He waited for everyone to nod in agreement, including Antoinette, who he looked at for a few long seconds to ensure he had her agreement. Apparently, she'd had words with him already.

"I went to my mother for advice, as you all know. She's been a Kabbalist for her entire life and has been teaching me long-distance. She took one look at me and popped me into a circle for a healing spell. It took her six tries of successively more powerful spells before she was able to crack the one that was on me. I'm not boasting when I say that I am one of the most powerful mages this coalition has working for them, but I had no idea at all that I had been enspelled. None. My mother and I both knew we needed to figure out what type of magic it was so I could learn to fight against it properly. It took us a day of research to realize neither of us had ever encountered this type of magic.

"But it wasn't the only magic I had been unable to identify. I remembered the spell that attacked Maki and Brandon, and I couldn't help wondering if maybe they were connected. I immediately recognized that some sort of voodoo or hoodoo had killed Randy the werebear. Mom called a friend in New Orleans who confirmed it, but insisted that the flies Yani saw and the centipede that Khan ate weren't anything she recognized. Mom and I were able to figure out pretty quickly that while hoodoo was definitely similar to the spell on me, it wasn't it exactly."

Aaron was talking earnestly, as if his explanation might erase his months of inactivity. It was nice to see Aaron so animated again, but Yani wasn't about to forget the months of hurt and abandonment. Yes, Aaron might have been under some sort of spell, but it had still been far too painful. Khan's warmth at Yani's back where he was standing was a helpful reminder of that.

"You see," Aaron continued doggedly, "voodoo and hoodoo are generally good, healing- and religious-type magics. Hollywood has portrayed them as evil, Satan-worshiping magic, but that was mostly influenced by ignorance and fear and isn't entirely true. There are dark practitioners, and Mom and I thought for a few moments that someone had summoned the evil loa Kalfu, but the strange bugs didn't fit. Then I remembered something

Khan had said: Who did I think had taught voodoo to the humans in the first place? Voodoo as we know it didn't originate in New Orleans. It came with the slaves captured in Africa and was changed by the influence of Christianity and Western ideals into what we now call voodoo.

"So I started researching about African magic, and I came upon something interesting. A large number of women in Saudi Arabia were having trouble with their maids hired from Morocco. The maids were using the magic they had learned at home in order to force the Saudi Arabian wives to leave their husbands so they could be married to rich men. One of those problems the maids caused was the wives were suddenly seeing strange insects meant to drive them from their homes.

"Cain summoned an ifrit, a creature from the Middle East, specifically the Arabian Peninsula, before. It stands to reason he would stick to the same region using dark magic he had probably taught to the people there hundreds of years ago."

It made sense to Yani, and he could see Luke nodding in agreement as well.

"So how does that help Maki?" Antoinette demanded.

"I know what magic I'm fighting against now, so I can target my healing spell," Aaron explained. "I think a gris-gris has been placed on us. Dark voodoo comes inherent with skepticism, mostly because the list of terrible things it can cause are both ridiculous and contradictory. For example, it can cause unwanted pregnancy, but it can also keep a woman barren. Yet, the list also states that a properly built gris-gris can cause apathy and isolationism, the two things I suddenly began suffering from. It can also cause stomach distress, exhaustion, and a sudden desire for infidelity," he added with a pointed look at Yani.

Yani frowned at Aaron. Sure, the first two described how he had been feeling lately, but there was no way it caused infidelity. Khan was a beautiful man with an engaging personality. Yani liked him, and that hadn't been caused by magic. Besides, Yani had broken up with Aaron already, so he wasn't being unfaithful.

"So you perform this healing spell and everyone walks away on two human feet?" Antoinette interrupted pointedly. Maki nodded her head behind her.

Aaron let out a breath. "I don't know. Maki and Brandon aren't injured—they're just blocked. I don't know if the healing spell will tear down that block entirely, or if it will weaken it enough that Maki and Brandon's willpower will be enough to finish destroying it. It will have at least a small, beneficial effect. I can promise that."

"Then hurry up and do the spell," Antoinette demanded.

Aaron cracked a smile at her, one that looked just like the smile he would have when he and Yani were first dating. "Of course," he told her. "This room was built with a protective circle around it already, so I should be able to just cast right here." He turned to look at Khan sharply. "Don't eat the magic in this spell. If you weaken it, it won't work at all."

"I promise I will not," Khan replied easily. He settled his hands protectively, and somewhat proprietarily, on Yani's shoulders. Aaron's eyes darkened at the sight, but he turned away to unroll the waiting scroll instead of saying anything.

"I call on the Seraphim," Aaron read. The scroll, which had been rolled a moment ago, now lay flat without anything holding it down. Aaron's hands were in the air in front of his face and blood was running from small cuts on the tips of both his pointer fingers.

"I call on the Seraphim," Aaron repeated. "Raphael, Seraph of healing, guide my steps. With Raphael behind me and Shekhinah above me, I call on you to guide my hands." Bright wings of light erupted from Aaron's back as they always did when he used the highest of his spells. Blood dripped from his hands onto the scroll below, and the wings grew even brighter, until Yani had to shade his eyes. "I call on the Seraphim! Provide healing to those in need, Raphael, Seraph of healing. Guide my will to help them!"

There was a brilliant flash of light that had Yani crying out in surprise. He ducked, but his vision was ruined. By the time he finished blinking away the dark spots, the scroll was rolled again, and Aaron was calmly blotting the blood off his fingers with a tissue.

"Did it work?" Antoinette demanded.

Yani took a breath and felt it go all the way into his lungs, deep, and felt his body open up as if he hadn't been capable of taking a full breath of air in weeks. His nausea and headache were gone, and the various aches and pains that had plagued his body had faded away as well.

"Something worked," Yani admitted.

Brandon was standing on his four paws, staring at Luke's still emaciated form and growling under his breath. Yani could almost see him straining, reaching for the will and the power to break through the spell holding him in wolf shape. His growls grew louder, forced out between clenched teeth as his muscles shook, and then with a sudden crack, he began to shift forms.

It was a grisly sight to see and hear. Bones snapped and reformed while muscle and ligaments shifted around under skin covered in receding fur. Yani had seen Brandon shift before, but it had never gone this slowly, as if it had been so long that each bone had to carefully remember how it was supposed to go. Brandon was howling in pain, and when his vocal chords changed, he started screaming instead. Luke was on his knees at Brandon's side with his hands held impotently over Brandon as if he didn't know what he could do to help. Yani didn't know what he could do either, but he was so glad to see Brandon finally returning to Luke.

The shift stopped as abruptly as it began, and Brandon panted weakly on the floor. His body was curled in a fetal position, but Yani thought he looked fully human. Brandon uncurled his body with a low groan that said things still ached, and then he looked up at Luke. With a growl that could only be described as sexual, Brandon leaped toward Luke. Their lips met with a wet smack, and Luke groaned in satisfaction.

"I need to feed," Luke whimpered, his hands circling around Brandon's back to dig his nails into Brandon's very human shoulder blades.

"So feed," Brandon growled back before licking a stripe down Luke's neck.

That was Yani's clue to leave. He headed to the door and was quickly followed by Khan, Aaron, Antoinette, and Maki, who was still in her panda form. The ripping sound of Luke's clothing being forcibly removed was cut off when the soundproof door to the practice room shut.

Maki sat on her hind legs so she could gently place one paw on Antoinette's shoulder. Antoinette looked up at her, and her face softened.

"Go ahead," Antoinette said softly. "I'll come by in twenty minutes to see if you need anything?" Maki nodded before ambling off. "She wants to try shifting in privacy," Antoinette explained as Maki hurried from view.

"When she's done, could you give her this?" Aaron asked, holding out a small white pouch for Antoinette to take. She gave him a suspicious look and opened the pouch to reveal Maki's sakura blossom necklace. "It's hers, and I think she'll want it back."

"Fine," Antoinette agreed. She closed the pouch again before turning sharply on one heel and hurrying after Maki.

Yani watched everything happening around him with a touch of awe. It was all so bright and vibrant where just five minutes ago it had felt like he was experiencing life though a thick shadow. He had no doubt that he had been cursed, and having it lifted was like seeing color for the first time.

"Can we talk? Alone?" Aaron asked Yani. He looked hopeful, yet resigned at the same time.

"I wish to also have a private conversation with both of you," Khan said, "but it can wait until tomorrow. Aaron, you are learning how to combat this Middle Eastern version of voodoo, and I wish to learn more. Yani, we are overdue for a conversation as well."

Yani swallowed hard and nodded. The curse hadn't just muted the world around him; it had muted his own emotions too. His heart was hurting again over Aaron, and his stomach was churning with worry over Khan. He hadn't been fully present in this world for far too long.

"Okay," Yani said in answer to them both.

Khan nodded and gave Yani a small smile that said he understood what had happened to Yani and would wait until they could properly talk before doing anything. He turned and walked off in the direction of the nearby gym, the opposite way Maki and Antoinette had gone. That left Yani alone with Aaron.

"I think this room is open too," Aaron said softly.

He led the way across the hall to another practice room and held the door open for Yani. He closed it sharply behind them and then took one of the seats around the small table in the middle of the room. Yani was slower to take his own seat, trying to figure out what he could say to Aaron that would erase both the hurt in his heart and the tense look on Aaron's face.

"I cried for two hours when my mom broke the gris-gris on me," Aaron said, his voice still soft and very gentle. "I missed you, and I knew I had lost you because I hadn't even noticed I was under a spell. How could I have allowed myself to hurt you like that?"

"It hurt a lot, Aaron," Yani finally said after a few seconds to gather his thoughts. "It still hurts. So many cold nights when the bed was empty, so many lifeless days while you ignored me. I had entire conversations with myself that you didn't even acknowledge. You don't know how lonely I was."

"All I can say is sorry, Yani. I am so unbelievably sorry. You relied on me to stay strong, to keep any magic from hurting us, and I was the first one to fall."

It did make sense. If Yani had started to suddenly act odd, Aaron would have noticed and figured out how to stop the spell months ago. With Aaron out of the picture, no one had been able to help them. In fact, once Aaron left, Yani had started to deteriorate. Only Khan's presence had kept Yani going these last few days.

And that was where Yani's uncertainty with the situation was coming from. He still loved Aaron, no doubt about that, but his heart was so very bruised. He couldn't fall back into Aaron's arms and pick up their relationship where it had left off before Aaron had been cursed. Yani couldn't do that even if he had never met Khan.

Yet Khan was also a factor. Yani didn't love Khan, but it was only a matter of time. Khan was a completely different person than Aaron in both personality and ability. He had supported Yani when Yani was down and was still there now that Yani was better. The truth was, Yani didn't want to lose what he had growing with Khan.

"Please, Yani. Will you forgive me?" Aaron asked, cutting into Yani's circling thoughts. His hands were reaching across the table in entreaty, and Yani couldn't help placing his right hand into Aaron's left.

It had been in one of these rooms that he and Aaron had first decided to see where their relationship would take them. They'd had their first kiss awkwardly leaning over one of these little tables. It was a sad irony that this same place was where their relationship would end.

"I understand you were affected by magic, Aaron," Yani forced out through a tight throat. He swallowed to clear it, but that only made the tears choking him swell. "I do, and I forgive you for what you couldn't control. But I'm hurting so much still." Yani couldn't help putting one hand over his chest where his heart was aching inside. His other hand wiped ineffectively at his face, but the tears wouldn't stop.

All those long days of loneliness, contrasted to Aaron now that he was free of the spell, and Yani couldn't jump back into where their relationship had left off. In some ways, he wanted to—desperately wanted to—fall back into Aaron's arms and that remembered happiness, but for every memory of them together was a more recent memory of Yani alone and in pain. Yes, knowing Aaron had been under a spell helped assuage his brain, but his heart remembered.

"I'm sorry, but I need space. I need time to myself to figure everything out and to let myself heal. I'm sorry."

Aaron's eyes were wet, too, as he pulled away. "I understand," he whispered, his own words also tight with suppressed emotion. "Maybe one day we can be friends again."

He stood and strode from the room before Yani could answer, leaving Yani alone to cry, yet again, over Aaron. This time the tears were healing. Aaron was gone, that stage of Yani's life over, and it was time to move on to something new. But...perhaps more slowly than he had been with Khan so far. He needed time to heal before jumping off the deep end again.

It was late when Yani finally stopped crying. He wiped his face on his sleeve to try to clear the worst of the evidence and then left the practice room to head to bed. The door across the hall was still closed, and Yani didn't dare peek inside to see how Luke and Brandon were doing.

Yani had to be at work in the morning, which was only a few hours from now. It wouldn't do to create a negative precedent by missing the first Friday at his new job. Julio was already unhappy that Yani had been sent to him.

He was exhausted from the long day and the crying, so Yani hurried through the long halls until he reached his dorm. Khan's bed was empty, but Yani wasn't worried. He didn't think Khan actually slept much. Yani got into his pajamas and crawled under the covers. He was asleep as soon as his head hit the pillow.

*

Yani woke and suddenly understood what people meant when they said they felt refreshed. It was amazing to wake up and not feel tired. He got ready for the day in record time and headed down to breakfast. He was suddenly in the mood for his favorite breakfast: scrambled eggs with a bagel thick with cream cheese, lox, and thinly sliced red onion. Unfortunately, the dining hall didn't offer that for breakfast, so Yani resigned himself to whatever they were serving that day.

"I already got you a plate," Khan said with a grin as he hurried over to Yani.

"Thanks." Yani followed Khan to a nearby table where two plates of steaming food were waiting for them. He saw scrambled eggs and a suspiciously thick bagel. Yani gaped at the food, then turned to look at Khan suspiciously.

"The mage told me you would want it," Khan explained with an unselfconscious shrug. That was very kind of Aaron, who had probably spent just as much time as Yani crying last night. "I also spoke to the chefs to complain about the lack of variety in their selections, particularly the fact that they serve bacon, sausage, hash, and raw steaks, but only offer soggy toast and burnt pancakes to anyone who doesn't eat pork."

Yani had nothing to say in response, but he really appreciated Khan's gesture. He sat and started eating. It was delicious. Creamy cheese had been melted into the eggs while they had cooked, and the lox was really fresh. It was even better than his mother's eggs, and that was saying something.

"Thank you, Khan," Yani said between bites.

"As I said, it was the mage's idea, and I find I am quite enjoying it." He took a large bite of his bagel to emphasize his words.

Yani didn't want to think about Aaron at the moment, so he returned to enjoying his breakfast. There wasn't as much time as he would have liked, so Yani couldn't savor it. It was a *schande*, a disgrace, but he had to get to work on time.

There was a lot more pep in his step when Yani headed into work. Even Julio looked up briefly as Yani walked past his desk. None of the files had been moved from where Yani had left them the previous afternoon. There were a few new ones left on one of the empty tables that Yani quickly organized before he returned to where he had left off sorting the Maine files.

It was still a chump job. Not even being fully present in his own life could change that fact. While it was tedious and mind-numbing, some of the stories were unbelievably interesting. It was probably the best window Yani had ever been given into the way the rest of the supernatural community lived. His little bubble amid the coalition's best had shielded him from some of the worst the supernatural community was capable of. The really bad ones were cut-and-dry cases, so his team had never been sent out. For example, something had slowly stripped each branch off a tree a dryad was using in the middle of Augusta, one of the busiest cities in the states, until the dryad had faded away. Few dryads could withstand the smog and muck of a dirty city, and someone had tortured it to death.

It wasn't the only case where a unique creature had been killed. Yani shuffled through his pile of sorted folders until he found another one. An encantado, a Brazilian shape-shifting dolphin, had been dragged out of Moosehead Lake and beaten to death. Alone, these cases looked like ordinary hate crimes, but put together on the same table, they told a different story.

There had also been the albino werewolf and the king cobra murders in Massachusetts, Yani remembered, and those were only the first of a few dozen he had filed over the last few days. It would have been easy enough to miss them hidden underneath the thousands of more ordinary crimes Yani had been filing, but he had gone to school for something like this. Halting discrimination that could lead to human rights violations had been the focus of quite a few of his classes, which also meant learning to recognize it whenever he encountered it.

There were almost a hundred magical creatures that had been brutally murdered, and each creature had been unique in some way. Creatures like Maki, a panda in a land of regular bears, or like Khan, the only dragon Yani had ever heard of, were the targets.

Yani scrambled across the room to the filing cabinets and started pulling the cases he remembered. He piled them on an empty table and yanked his phone out of his pocket.

He had thirty-two missed calls and six messages. Yani swiped past them to get to Luke's number.

"What's up?" Luke asked, sounding chipper and perfectly healthy again.

"I've found something," Yani said in a rush, adrenaline pumping as he dug through the ongoing files for New Hampshire. "I can't believe I missed it!"

"What is it?" Luke replied.

"Someone's killing creatures, and I think there's a pattern," Yani explained. "Can you grab one of the conference rooms? And call everyone in. I think Cain's up to something terrible."

"I'm on it," Luke said immediately.

Yani put his phone back in his pocket so he would have both hands free to carry the large stack of folders he had compiled. He had to fumble for the door and then balance his folders as he hurried from the room and out into the chaos of the administrative offices. Somehow, he made it through without dumping everything.

"Where do you think you're going with those files?" Julio gasped when he caught sight of Yani. "Those are confidential and need to be kept in their proper cabinets!"

"I'll explain later!" Yani called over his shoulder as he hurried out the door. Luckily, the conference rooms were on this side of the building, only two floors up, and Yani hurried into the closest one. Luke and Brandon were only a few minutes behind. It took Aaron and Khan a few more minutes to join them.

"What did you find?" Aaron asked, immediately getting to business.

"I found these," Yani said with a grand gesture toward the pile of folders. "There are thousands of files covering everything under the sun, but among the dreck were some cases that jumped out at me. Each one of these is a brutal murder, often with torture involved." Yani pulled the first file off the top of the stack and found the albino werewolf case. "An albino werewolf was skinned alive and left to die." The second folder below that was the king cobra shifter. "A king cobra was stabbed repeatedly in a back alley in Springfield."

"So there are a lot of murders," Luke said with an offhand shrug. "Us supernatural creatures tend to be a fairly violent bunch."

"What the heck was a king cobra doing in Springfield?" Aaron asked before Yani could formulate a reply to Luke.

"That's what I'm saying," Yani explained. "Each one of these creatures is totally unique: a king cobra in Springfield, an encantado in Maine, a panda in Bolton Landing."

"Or a dragon," Khan added softly. "You think my hoard was bombed, not as a diversion so they could kill Randy, but rather that my violent death was always part of the plan?"

"Or even setting the coalition on one of the few leprechauns left in the world." Yani knew the coalition would have been far more severe in their punishment of

Martlestiltskin had he not also been a victim. "What better way to torture a leprechaun than to have their carefully stored power forcibly taken from them?"

"What on earth is going on here?" Bishop asked sternly from the doorway. Everyone jumped in surprise and turned to look at him. "Luke left me a cryptic message on my phone, and then I received a frantic call that Yani had stolen important documents from Julio. Now I find you plotting something? Should I be worried?"

Bishop was only partially joking. Brandon was his grandson, and he had personally hired Yani and Aaron. He knew Yani wouldn't have taken the files without cause. Still, having his work interrupted because they were making a scene was reason enough to take them to task.

"Yani found something," Brandon explained. "In the filing room."

"What were you doing in the filing room?" Bishop asked Yani curiously. "I thought Julio had a team working in there to keep the room straight."

Yani didn't want to badmouth his new boss, but it sounded like Julio had been cutting corners. If Yani hadn't stumbled on the pattern, no one might ever have, and they wouldn't have this clue to finding Cain.

"The filing room looked like it hadn't been touched in months," Yani said, trying to be delicate while knowing he was failing. "I was sorting through the tables of files when I started seeing a pattern in many of the creatures being murdered. Each one of these"—he pointed toward his stack of folders—"is an extremely violent murder of a creature unique to this part of the world. A king cobra shifter was killed, an albino werewolf, an encantado, all of which were different from the norm in New England."

"And you think Cain is behind it?" Bishop asked. He looked thoughtful instead of skeptical, so Yani forged on.

"I do. When he captured us two years ago, we learned that he likes to kill creatures so he can steal their magic. Some of the creatures in this stack had to be inordinately strong to survive in these adverse circumstances. The encantado was living in a fresh water lake before he was beaten to death, and dolphins are usually saltwater mammals."

"You think you can figure out where he's going to strike next," Bishop guessed correctly. "Are these all the files?"

"Only the ones I could carry. I haven't even started going through the pile for Albany."

"We need to finish establishing the pattern, see if we can narrow down his next target. For that, we will need all the files we have that fit this criteria." Bishop frowned at them all before nodding to himself. "Yani, lead the way."

Yani quickly gathered up his stack of files again and headed back out the door and down the stairs. It had only been ten minutes since he had left, but this time he felt like he had a real purpose again. The drive to figure out where the bad guys were hiding and the preparation to confront them was extremely exhilarating. Yani couldn't believe he had given it up—not working with his team to stop the evil in the world clearly wasn't an option. He would need to figure out a way to handle working with Aaron now that they weren't in a relationship, but Yani wasn't willing to give up his job anymore.

"You!" Julio snarled as soon as Yani stepped into the administrative offices. He pointed a finger at Yani as if that would pin him in place so Julio could berate him.

Yani ignored him, instead walking past and through the rows of desks that led to the filing room.

Julio opened his mouth to shout at Yani again, but he snapped it shut again as Aaron and Khan strode into the room, following Yani. Their faces were both set in straight frowns that made them look serious and slightly dangerous. Brandon and Luke were right on their heels, and somehow Brandon's flyaway hair and Luke's colorful tattoos only emphasized their thinking this situation might be dire. Julio would have still yelled—Yani could see him girding himself—but then Bishop strode into the room directly behind them all with his own very serious frown on his face. Bishop followed them toward the records room, and Julio sank back down into his chair without speaking.

The fingerprint scanner accepted Yani's finger, and the door popped open. Yani held it so everyone could get inside, but when Bishop reached the door, something, probably a spell, caused the door to open all the way and stay that way.

"I need every file that pertains to our research," Bishop said, even as Yani was already pulling open the nearest filing cabinet to go through more ongoing cases. "Brandon, you and Luke start with the Albany files that aren't sorted yet. Who were you working with in here, Yani?" Bishop asked Yani in a much less authoritative voice.

Yani looked up at Bishop in surprise. "No one?" he said curiously, wondering what Bishop was talking about. "All six tables were covered in files and dust. I've been getting it all organized over the past week."

"Interesting," Bishop said sharply, his eyes blazing as he spoke. His ire wasn't for Yani, though. "If you'll excuse me," he said before striding back out the door.

The door remained open, and a few moments later, Yani could hear Bishop's raised voice through the doorway.

"I sent you one of my finest investigators to join your department and you put him on filing?" Bishop hissed. The question was clearly redundant, and Julio didn't even try to blubber out on answer. "Which I find particularly interesting, as according to the monthly finances the coalition provides for this department, there are ten employees that work exclusively in the filing room. Yet, it's clear that no one worked there until you forced Yani to do their job. I expressly told you that part of this department's duties was to read through every single investigation file and look for patterns between multiple cases that my investigators working on singular cases would have missed. Why hasn't this important task been completed?"

Bishop paused as if to give time for Julio to answer. Yani couldn't hear one from his distance away, so either Julio wasn't yelling or, as Yani suspected, he didn't have an answer.

"Very well," Bishop continued. "You are being put on unpaid administrative leave until such a time as you can come forward with an answer. I will have an auditor here this afternoon to go through this department's finances to see where all the extra money has gone, and I will have someone from my own office here at the same time to go through your personnel files to double check your policies for hiring and firing your employees.

"This entire office is dismissed for today!" Bishop added in an even louder voice. "Reroute the phone lines to my office for now. All of you, except Julio, will report back here on Monday as usual. Have a pleasant weekend."

Chairs scraped on the floor, and a great rustle of clothing and papers drowned out anything else Bishop might have said. Yani barely knew Julio, so he couldn't be happy or sad that he was in trouble. However, had someone been doing the job Julio had coldly forced Yani to do, how much sooner would the pattern Yani had noticed been found? How many of the deaths Yani and his friends were pulling out of the cabinets could have been prevented had they been able to confront Cain months ago? And, more significant to Yani, would Cain have ever had the chance to put a gris-gris on Aaron and Yani, thereby ruining their happy relationship and putting a terrible strain on all their friends?

Yani pushed those thoughts away. They weren't what was important at the moment—figuring out the pattern and where Cain would strike next was. Preferably before he had the chance to kill again.

"Is anyone searching the completed files to see if anyone survived a violent attack?" Bishop asked as he walked back into the room. "The survivors might be able to give us some insight."

"In all my research about Cain, the only survivors I've been able to find up until now are the four of us," Aaron said with a wave toward Yani, Luke, and Brandon. "He doesn't leave witnesses. In fact, if Yani's right, and he did trick the coalition into going after Martlestiltskin and we refused to execute him, he probably finished the job. I'll bet there's a recent folder in the New Hampshire section on his death."

"I didn't see it," Yani admitted. "But I wasn't looking for names, just whether the case was still ongoing or not. If it didn't jump out at me, I might not have noticed."

"I'll check," Luke said, leaving Brandon alone with the unsorted Albany files to open up the cabinets for New Hampshire.

"If this Cain of yours never misses his kills, what do you suppose he might do after having missed both Maki and me?" Khan asked.

That made Yani pause, his hands still over the next file he had been about to open.

"He would find a way to target you to finish the job," Aaron replied with horror dawning on his face. "Has anyone spoken with Maki since yesterday evening?"

Everyone's head shook a no.

"She's living in the vampire house," Brandon interjected. "That's almost as safe as the coalition building, right?"

"It used to be," Bishop disagreed. "But there are so few vampires living there at the moment that it would be possible to slip someone or something in. I've had to preventatively strengthen the protections on the tunnels linking the vampire house to the coalition."

Yani could see his own horror on everyone else's faces. Maki, that sweet panda, might need their help.

"Go!" Bishop ordered. "I have people coming to help me here. Go ensure Maki and all the vampires are safe."

They all dropped whatever they were holding and ran.

*

Antoinette wanted to hurry after Maki, to hold her hand through the violent shift from panda to human, but she knew Maki wanted her privacy. It was personal to have your body twisted inside out and have one living creature replace another. Maki would return to human naked, which Antoinette did want to see, but in totally different circumstances. She wanted Maki to feel comfortable enough with Antoinette as a human as well as a panda. It would take time, so Antoinette respected Maki's wishes to be allowed to shift forms in peace.

Antoinette quickly returned to the vampire house, but instead of rushing upstairs to Maki's side like she wanted, Antoinette paced back and forth through the downstairs rooms. She was waiting for Maki to call down to say she was okay, but the call never came.

Ten minutes became twenty and twenty became thirty before Antoinette ran out of patience. She bounded up the flight of stairs, skipping steps in her haste, and hurried to Maki's closed bedroom door. She paused outside the door to listen for a few moments, but there was only silence on the other side.

"Maki?" Antoinette called out and knocked gently on the door. "Is everything okay? Can I come in?"

She heard a grunt through the door, and her heart sank. That wasn't a noise a human could make, but a bear could. Antoinette slowly pushed the door open and wasn't surprised to see Maki still in her panda form sitting in the center of the room.

"Oh, Maki," Antoinette breathed out. She hurried forward and dropped to her knees at Maki's side.

Maki's cheeks were dry, but her eyes were wide and her paws shaking as if she were in shock. Antoinette carefully wrapped her arms around Maki's massive shoulders and pulled her into a hug.

"The mage did say his spell would only weaken the block," Antoinette murmured. "You just need a bit more time to figure out how to get through it."

Maki grunted pointedly, and Antoinette took a wild guess about the direction of her thoughts.

"Did you see the werewolf's mate? The incubus looked like he was only hours from death. That kind of incentive would have driven him to lengths even he probably didn't know he could go to in order to regain control over his wolf form. That's what we need to find for you," Antoinette said firmly. "We need to find something you desperately care about that will enable you to reach that extra step and change forms again. That's all."

Maki grunted again, but her shoulders shuddered under Antoinette's arms as she finally dissolved into tears.

"We will figure it out together," Antoinette insisted again. "I won't leave you until we do."

Maki rested her head against Antoinette's. She was heavy and furry, but the sensation of the weight and the gentle brush of soft fur was probably the very best thing Antoinette had ever felt in her very long and difficult life. She lifted one hand and ran it down the fur on the back of Maki's head, stroking her comfortingly as Maki cried.

Antoinette didn't keep track of the clock, but she felt stiff from sitting on the floor with a heavy panda on top of her by the time Maki's tears dried. Maki slowly pulled away and then shifted her body until she was on her knees. She bowed low to the floor, facing Antoinette, with her paws carefully placed before her body. It was probably the only way she could express her gratitude in her current form.

"There is no need to thank me," Antoinette insisted. "I want to do this for you, with you, and I think it will be an interesting fight to get you whole again. Don't ever feel indebted to me."

Maki sat up again, and the arch of her eyebrow told Antoinette that she couldn't obey Antoinette's demand. Still, it was clear she was at least willing to try.

"Before I forget, Aaron gave me this to give to you." Antoinette pulled the beautiful necklace out of her pocket and held it out for Maki to see. Maki sucked in a shocked breath, and one trembling claw reached out to touch the sakura charm as if to double-check it was actually real. She pulled her claw away abruptly and shook her head, pushing Antoinette's hand away with one paw as if to say she couldn't deal with it at the moment. Antoinette tucked the necklace back into her pocket. When Maki was human again, Antoinette would try then, but it was clearly too much for Maki to handle right now.

"So, I say we go find ourselves some dinner first," Antoinette said briskly. She stood and then held out a hand for Maki to take. Maki took it, but she didn't use Antoinette to climb to her feet. The soft pads and the prick of her sharp nails against Antoinette's hand only served to reiterate Antoinette's desire to feel the touch of Maki's human hand in hers as well. "After dinner, we'll go find the mage and ask him for advice. He was able to help the werewolf, so maybe he'll have a stronger spell to try on you."

Maki nodded and let Antoinette lead her to the door. Antoinette stepped into the hallway first, but then waited for Maki to duck and turn so she could fit through also. They went down the stairs still holding hands and headed to the front door.

"My, how big you've gotten," a man's voice purred from the direction of the stairs to the basement. "The little girl, all grown up. I know someone who would be very interested to learn how you managed to suddenly grow in power."

Antoinette thought she recognized the voice, but as she spun around to look, she couldn't see anyone. She strained her eyes into the night-darkened shadows and could just barely make out the outline of a man through the gloom.

"What do you want?" Antoinette asked. Only a vampire magically tied into the wards—and now Maki as well—could get through the protections on the house. There were so few vampires left in the house that she should have been immediately able to place this one, but she couldn't.

"It's not about what I want. Not anymore. It's about what the one who sent me here wants, and he wants her head." A long finger with a pointed nail became visible as the man extended his arm in Maki's direction. "She was supposed to have been brutally killed by her fellow bears, but they instead turned to the coalition," he scoffed. "Well, I've been sent to rectify that mistake."

The man slowly stepped out of the shadow, as if by taking his time he could paralyze them with fear. Once the ambient light from the moon overhead and the lights from the nearby buildings hit his face, Antoinette immediately recognized him. Except, it wasn't the vampire she used to know.

"You were the coven master before me," she said, stalling for time to think of an escape route even as she stepped between him and Maki.

He didn't look like a normal vampire. His skin was sallow and pasty, like a decaying corpse rather than the living dead. His black hair, once his favorite feature, which he would spend hours primping and brushing, was falling out in large chunks, leaving behind glistening bald patches.

"I am still the master of this coven!" he hissed. "I am Felipe, the strongest vampire in the entire Northeast! Obey me, child, and give this creature to the death I have been ordered to provide."

"If you are the strongest vampire, Felipe, then why are you obeying someone else's orders?" Antoinette asked. Felipe was blocking the front door and the entrance to the basement where the tunnel to the coalition building was located. Their only hope to escape him was the back door, so Antoinette angled herself so she could push Maki in the right direction.

"Oh, do run," Felipe said joyfully, ignoring Antoinette's words in favor of her actions. "I love the chase and the hunt. It is always so much sweeter when I catch and kill my prey."

He leaped without warning, arcing through the air as if he could jump over Antoinette entirely and land on Maki. For such a large creature, Maki was swift. She dodged to the side without needing Antoinette's warning shout and spun around to keep Felipe in sight.

Antoinette was the weakest coven leader New England had ever seen. Most of the vampires had fled to stronger leaders in other parts of the world where they could feel protected. A vampire was most vulnerable during the day when sleep overcame the weaker ones, and the sunlight kept even the strongest confined indoors, and they wanted a master who could ensure their safety. She was nothing in comparison to what Felipe had been. Antoinette knew she couldn't defeat him, but she also couldn't watch while he killed Maki. She had to do something, so she leaped at him with her fangs bared.

Felipe didn't notice her until after she had clawed up his side and bitten deep into his shoulder to remove a large chunk of flesh. She would take him apart piece by piece if that would keep Maki safe. Felipe flung her off with one arm. She braced for impact against the wall and used the momentum to leap for him again. Felipe had already forgotten about her, instead turning on Maki with a single-mindedness that Antoinette was hoping to exploit. Except he spun just as she was about to land and backhanded her across the face so hard her body flew into another wall.

Stunned, it took her a few seconds to shake off the figurative birdies circling her head and stumble back to her feet.

Maki let out a roar as she grappled with Felipe, holding him off with her claws. She'd had some martial arts training in the past, Antoinette could see from her carefully balanced stance, but it translated differently between a human body and a panda. Felipe was able to get under her guard and score a line of claw marks down her tender stomach. Maki let out a gasp of pain, and Antoinette rushed Felipe.

She kept low this time, running at him instead of jumping, and was able to surprise him with another gouged-out piece of flesh. He didn't seem to feel the pain, though, easily flinging Antoinette away yet again.

"It seems I will have to deal with you first, child," Felipe said as he glared at Antoinette.

She got to her feet and returned his glare. "I don't think you can handle me," she hissed.

"Ha! Child, the little power you have managed to gain in my absence has made you foolish."

No, the need to keep Maki safe had made her foolish, but she wasn't about to tell him that. She rushed him again, but he vanished in a blur of speed she couldn't follow. His claws hooked into her shoulder, the exact same spot she had first injured him, and ripped out a line of flesh down her arm.

Antoinette barely held in a shriek as her arm immediately went numb and hung uselessly at her side.

"Shall I remove a leg next or incapacitate your other arm?" Felipe was smiling as he spoke, enjoying watching her bleed. She couldn't give him the satisfaction.

"I think more of your hair fell out," she hissed through teeth clenched against the pain.

One of his hands instinctively reached for the top of his head, but he stopped it before he could touch it. Then he vanished again in a blur of speed. Antoinette kicked out, hoping she could hit him, and missed. A hand grabbed her around the throat and lifted her into the air. Her back slammed against the nearest wall so hard all the air was forced from her lungs.

"You dare make fun of me? Me! Felipe, the strongest vampire in the world? Let's see how hard you can laugh when I rip out your vocal cords!"

The hand around her throat tightened, his claws digging deep into her neck. Blood flowed. She could feel it dampening her shirt and dripping down her torso. Antoinette refused to cry, but she could feel her death coming.

Maki roared, and Felipe's eyes widened in shock. Antoinette could feel Maki's claws pressing against her stomach. Maki had dug deep into Felipe's body and, with another roar, she yanked. With a sound like wet paper tearing in two, Felipe's body was pulled away from Antoinette. She fell to the ground weakly and knew she had already lost too much blood.

There was a thump, and she turned her head to the left and saw a pair of legs from the hips down land on the floor. Another thump and she turned her head in the other direction to see the rest of Felipe's body. Maki had torn him in half.

Maki dropped to her knees at Antoinette's side with a pained gasp. Her bloody claws hovered over Antoinette as if she didn't know what she could do to help.

Antoinette coughed and felt blood dribble down her chin. "I need fresh blood," she forced out, stuttering and stumbling over her words. "To heal. Run to. Run to...coalition. Get blood." Antoinette ran out of strength to continue, and her eyes slid shut. She felt Maki's warmth move away and knew Maki was probably running for help. It would take too long for her to get to the coalition, find someone able to help, and get back. Antoinette would be long gone by then, but at least she knew Maki wouldn't have to watch her die. It was a small mercy, one she couldn't help cherishing as she felt her consciousness begin to fade.

There was a terrible cracking sound, and then another and another. Felipe probably wasn't dead and was punching holes into the floor as he dragged what was left of his body over to hers to ensure she died too. Antoinette didn't have the strength to open her eyes and see.

Bleeding out was a slow way to die. She remembered seeing it a few times as a slave when the master's whip had scored too deeply and a slave had been left to bleed nourishment into the earth the crops grew on. It was even slower as a vampire, since she didn't have a beating heart to pump the blood out. The magic that circulated her blood was slower, and it gave her time to wish the best for Maki in the future. Surely the mage would be willing to try another spell to help her become human.

Warm flesh was pushed into Antoinette's mouth. Her body reacted instinctively, her vampiric need for blood forcing her teeth to close on that flesh and draw out fresh blood.

It flowed like mulled wine, rich and potent across her tongue. Fresh, fresher than anything she thought she had ever tasted. Strength returned slowly. She was able to suckle at the flesh within a few moments, and after a minute, she could lift her uninjured hand to press the flesh deeper into her mouth.

The skin on Antoinette's neck started knitting back together with a tingling feeling that made her want to itch it, but her injured arm was still useless at her side. Her eyes opened slowly, and she looked down at the wrist in her mouth. It was attached to a supple arm, which led Antoinette's eyes to a very naked woman's body. The woman's head was bowed, her silky dark hair covering her face, but Antoinette knew who this was.

She pulled the wrist from her mouth, carefully licking the puncture marks to seal the wounds from her fangs.

"Maki," Antoinette whispered and had to cough to clear her throat. "Maki, you're human."

Maki slowly lifted her head so Antoinette could see her face. Her eyes were the same as in her panda form, large and dark and beautiful. She was crying again, but her tears dried the moment she saw Antoinette's smile.

"You're alive," Maki whispered back.

"And healing, thanks to you," Antoinette added with a pointed wiggle of the now-mobile fingers on her broken arm. "Did I take too much blood?"

"It comes back," Maki replied in a stronger voice. She was a were, Antoinette remembered, with superior healing. She could handle Antoinette's feeding better than most.

Antoinette lifted her good arm so her fingers could gently stroke down the tear streaks on Maki's cheeks.

"You're human," Antoinette stated again.

Maki nodded, ducking her head shyly even as she pressed closer to Antoinette's fingers. "Like you said, seeing someone you love, your mate, moments from death is a very good motivator. I needed to be human to help you, so I found where my human form had been hiding and forced it back to the fore of my body again." She smiled happily, looking down at her human fingers and curling them to show her human nails. There was blood imbedded underneath them and splashed across her pert little breasts, probably from Felipe, since it didn't smell fresh.

"You should shower and find some clothing," Antoinette murmured. It was a shame she was too injured to take advantage of the moment, but they would have time in the future.

"I'm not leaving you lying on the floor to heal," Maki replied indignantly. "You said you have a room below ground? Show me where it is." Maki's arms slid underneath Antoinette's body, and with a delicate grunt, she lifted Antoinette into the air and climbed to her feet. That amount of strength and power in this woman was unbelievably exhilarating, but again, Antoinette was still too injured to do anything about it. For now, she reminded herself. With a bit more blood and a full day's rest, that would change.

Instead, Antoinette enjoyed the moment as she directed Maki into the basement.

Chapter Four

Battle

They were on the ground level floor of the coalition building, which was the only good thing Yani could say about the situation. It still took some time to reach a door that led in the direction of the vampire house. They ran across the uneven ground of the forest that separated the two houses, Yani desperately trying not to trip over an exposed root or a dip in the earth. Brandon, the fastest of them, was in the lead, with Khan just on his heels. Aaron exercised regularly and wasn't puffing too hard, but the only exercise Yani regularly got was with his martial arts instructor. She had gone back to Japan to visit her family for two months, and practicing on his own just wasn't the same. Luke was panting just as hard at Yani's side. The only exercise Yani assumed Luke got was between the sheets with Brandon. There wasn't time for small talk, so Yani fixed his eyes on the house they were approaching.

Brandon and Khan stopped just inside the tree line where they were hidden from view of the house to wait for everyone to catch up.

"There aren't enough of us for a proper assault," Brandon said just loud enough to be heard over Yani and Luke panting desperately for breath. "We'll have to go in the front door as one force and hope they don't drag Maki out the back."

"Agreed," Aaron murmured. "Do we go upstairs or down?"

"Downstairs," Brandon replied firmly, without hesitation. "If any vampires are alive, they'll be downstairs."

"But Maki isn't a vampire," Yani gasped out, still out of breath. He tried to purposefully breathe slowly to get himself under control again, but he knew he needed to hit a treadmill regularly from now on. It wasn't acceptable to be in such bad shape, given his job's stringent requirements. The last few months had really taken their toll on him.

"But if she ran, it would be to Antoinette, where she could get help," Aaron said, agreeing with Brandon.

They waited another minute to survey the house and to see if there was any movement in the windows, but they were all closed and covered by shades. It was too difficult to make out anything, so they would have to go in blind.

"Let's do this," Luke insisted.

Aaron and Brandon looked at each other to make sure they were ready, then nodded to everyone else.

"We go in first. I shield, and Brandon attacks. Khan, I want you at our backs, ready with an attack spell. Luke, you're with Khan. Drop anyone that attacks us into dreams and keep an eye on our backs. Yani, watch our backs as well and keep an eye out for spells or illusions we can't see." This was the Aaron Yani remembered and loved. His take-charge attitude and his confidence were unbelievably sexy... And not Yani's to savor anymore. They had broken up, and Yani had something interesting with Khan just beginning to bud.

Yani needed to put his mixed emotions aside. They had to save Maki first, and then he needed to go somewhere with Khan and have that talk Khan kept insisting on. Then, maybe, Yani could finally get naked and have sex. It had been so frigging long since he had anything more than his own hand in the shower. And he was distracted again. Yani refocused on the here and now by mentally telling his libido to shut the hell up.

Everyone was set, so they all turned toward the house. Aaron and Brandon left the tree line first, running directly to the front door and plastering themselves to either side. There was a light glow around Aaron that sparkled slightly, which meant he was ready to cast a spell. Luke and Khan left the trees when Aaron and Brandon were safely hidden against the house and able to watch them closely. Yani stuck to their heels, unwilling to wait by himself. He was the weakest of them all in terms of magical and physical strength, but his eyes had proven themselves to be invaluable over and over again. He was a part of this team, something he had unfortunately forgotten and wouldn't allow himself to forget ever again.

Once everyone was safely out of sight against the house, Brandon glanced at Yani to double-check that Yani didn't see any spells or traps on the door before carefully reaching out to grip the doorknob. With his free hand, he counted down with his fingers—three...two...one—and then threw the door open. Aaron went inside first, his shield spell blazing in Yani's sight, and Brandon followed him. Brandon's hands were still human, but they had what looked like an extra joint, and his nails were extremely sharp. He had learned how to partially shift specific parts of his body, a skill most weres were never able to learn. Luke went next, and Khan followed with Yani tight on his heels.

Yani glanced around the room but didn't see anything that looked like a spell or an illusion. The room was dark thanks to the heavy curtains that draped all the windows. Just enough light filtered through that Yani could see, although absolute darkness wouldn't hide magic from his sight. Two people were lying on the floor, Yani noticed as he carefully put his back to the wall by the door where he could keep an eye on everything. Actually, it was only one person. A pair of legs were lying closest to Yani, and he could just make out the torso across the room.

"It's Felipe," Brandon hissed in a low tone. He crouched down by the head of the torso, but he didn't touch. There was something not quite right with the torso.

Yani glanced at Luke to alert him he was moving from his place by the door. Luke stepped back to take Yani's spot as Yani carefully crossed the room to Brandon's side.

"It's empty," Yani gasped. He bent down where the body had been ripped in half, looking up into a rib cage that should have still held intestines and organs adapted by magic to synthesize blood. Yani could see all the way up to where a shriveled object that might be the heart lay.

"Someone sucked out the essence of what this vampire once was and then filled the shell with enough animus to pilot it," Khan explained. He sounded shocked that someone would do such a thing, but Yani knew not to ever doubt the cruelty of Cain. "And then it appears a bear tore him apart."

"Maki must have defended herself," Brandon agreed. "It couldn't have been hard once she got her claws into him since there was only a bit of skin and bone holding him together."

"So where is Maki now?" Aaron asked. "We need to continue our search."

Brandon stiffened and held up a hand. Everyone froze in place, and Yani followed the direction of Brandon's gaze to see a closed door off to the right. Khan heard whatever Brandon had a moment later, but it was a few more seconds before Yani could make out the gentle tap of footsteps climbing stairs. Yani backed away until he was against the wall again and saw a wave of sparkles as Aaron prepared himself for whatever was coming.

The door opened slowly, and a small Asian woman wearing a tightly belted, oversized bathrobe stepped into the room.

"It's been hours since the attack," she scolded with a disappointed frown. "Did no one at the coalition building hear our screams?" Her voice was all-American, but there was a lyrical note to her vowels that said English wasn't her only language.

"Maki, it's too far away to hear anything properly, even with our ears," Brandon said soothingly. She must smell the same as a panda, which was why Brandon was able to identify her so easily. Maki probably hadn't known to contact the coalition for help after the attack. Brandon's hands had dropped to his sides, which meant he didn't think there was a threat. Aaron followed Brandon's cue, letting the magic he had gathered dissipate harmlessly. "Are you okay?"

"I have healed," she said. She stepped farther into the room now that she knew they weren't going to attack her. "Antoinette could use some more blood, but she is sleeping at the moment. When she wakes at dusk, she will need to feed again."

"I smell you," a voice said ominously from behind them. "I will hunt you to the end of days, as I have been ordered!"

Yani looked away from Maki toward the voice and saw the upper half of Felipe's body sit up as if it still had abdominal muscles attached. It then stood up even though its legs were across the room, hovering in the air.

"I can't see the magic that's controlling it," Yani said quickly, squinting through the dark at the body. There had to be a spell of sorts, or at least strings of magic controlling it, but try as he might, Yani couldn't find anything.

"But can you hear it?" Khan asked.

A strange sort of tingling feeling ran through Yani's body—magic of some sort that felt like Khan—and suddenly, faintly, Yani could hear something strange.

"It's howling," Yani whispered. Exactly like how a thousand voices shrieking from the depths of hell should sound: high-pitched and in desperate pain. "Felipe is trapped in the shell, forced to obey," Yani deciphered, but he wasn't hearing everything the voices were saying. "There are dozens of vampires trapped in there, probably all the ones we could never locate at the hunter's compound two years ago. They just want the freedom to be allowed to die." The sound was probably the worst Yani had ever heard.

"So let's let them die," Aaron said calmly. He glowed suddenly in Yani's sight and flung out his arms. Streams of magic erupted, hitting the heavy curtains on the windows and yanking them open. Sunlight filled the room with brilliance.

The body of Felipe screamed out its defiance, but the howling of the trapped souls faded away. The abandoned legs disintegrated first, turning into ash almost immediately. The magic holding Felipe together withstood the sun a few moments longer, but even it couldn't keep a vampire together against the power of the sun. Ashes rained down to pile on the floor until nothing was left.

Aaron knelt at the side of the pile and reached into his pocket to pull out a pair of rubber gloves. He put the gloves on, then pulled out a stack of cloth bags from the same pocket, a pocket that remained suspiciously flat. Aaron scooped the pile of ashes into six separate bags before moving to the legs and putting those ashes into two bags. He then carefully removed his gloves and put them in one final bag.

"Bishop will have the bags emptied in separate bodies of water across the world. By the time any of the ashes reunite, there won't be enough magic left for the body to reform. All the trapped vampires will safely pass on to the afterlife."

"So it's safe here?" Maki asked. She didn't look tired, but there was a weight to her voice that spoke of exhaustion.

"Let me call Bishop and ask what he wants to do," Aaron said.

He pulled his phone from that same suspiciously flat pocket and hit one of his speed dial numbers. It took him a few minutes to explain the situation once Bishop answered, and then Aaron listened silently for a few more minutes before hanging up.

"Bishop will post guards around the vampire house for the rest of the day. He will have rooms in the coalition prepared for all the vampires living here. Maki, you need to tell Antoinette to tell those vampires about the change in quarters. We have some of your clothes to change into, but Bishop is also having some more overnighted from your home so you don't have to remain in a bathrobe. You should have your own things by tomorrow morning." Aaron turned to everyone else in the room before continuing. "Bishop has his own people looking through the files, but he says the more eyes we have, the better. We should all return to the filing room as soon as everything is settled down here."

It was only a few minutes of waiting before someone politely knocked on the front door before opening it. Aaron seemed to recognize the man because he walked over to talk. Brandon went over to Maki.

"Are you okay? The shift back was really hard for me, but I actually think I gained a level of power over my wolf by doing it. I can shift individual parts of my body now," he told her.

"And when he shifts his dick bigger, let me tell you," Luke murmured into Yani's ear with a low, happy growl.

"I haven't really checked yet," Maki admitted to Brandon. "I'm a bit afraid to call on my panda again. What if I get stuck?"

"So, anything more happening between you and dragon-boy?" Luke asked, interrupting Yani's eavesdropping.

"No," Yani admitted with a sigh. "He says we need to talk first before anything more happens, but there isn't any time to talk. We're going to spend all of today and probably most of tonight in the filing room and be so exhausted afterward that we'll only be able to sleep, and then tomorrow we'll either still be looking through files or running off to get ready to confront Cain before he can kill again."

"So after things settle down again then?" Luke asked with a cheeky smile. "I'll have to remember to ask for details."

Yani rolled his eyes and turned back to the conversation Brandon and Maki were having. Luke laughed and walked off.

"I think you'll find," Brandon was telling Maki, "that you're now much more in touch with your panda half. Shifting forms will be faster and more painless, and you won't ever have trouble finding your human self while a panda. I don't think a spell like the one that first caught us will ever catch us again, to be honest."

"That is comforting to know," Maki admitted. "But that doesn't stop the fear."

"You won't know until you change shape again," Brandon said. "Just remember that if you do get stuck, we're all here to help you."

"I appreciate that," Maki said. "I should get back to Antoinette. Thank you for coming to our rescue, even if it was a few hours late."

"Call if you need something else," Brandon insisted. "Blood will be sent over tonight for Antoinette."

Maki bowed briefly before turning and heading back down the stairs to the basement.

"All right, we're cleared to head back to the coalition," Aaron called. "I guess that means we're back to reading through files again."

"I suppose so," Khan sighed. "At least this is far more interesting than being alone in my cave. I shall have to reevaluate my quarters once this issue has been dealt with." He led the way back outside and through the forest. Everyone followed, and within a few minutes they were walking back through the halls of the coalition toward the administration offices.

The room was still empty when they got there, although on second glance, Yani noticed a few desks were occupied, but not by their original owners. Bishop must have his people investigating everything in the office to see what else Julio had been up to. The filing room wasn't empty. People were already sitting around the long tables with chairs that had materialized from somewhere, digging through mountains of files.

"Where do you need us?" Yani asked Bishop, who was supervising as well as going through his own stack of folders.

"That table," Bishop said, pointing to the second table along the row where only two people were sitting. "Actually, just find an empty chair anywhere and start reading. I've got enough people pulling files and putting them back; I need you to go through them."

They all found empty chairs, and Yani pulled the closest stack of files over to him to start reading. Hours passed. Every once in a while, Yani would have to pause to rub his eyes or stand up to walk in a circle around the tables to stretch his legs. He had found maybe one case about a were-buffalo that had been killed, but the hit-and-run circumstances didn't quite fit. He was looking at cases that were almost two years old, though, and it seemed Cain hadn't started killing until about nine months ago. It had escalated in the last month and half, which was why Yani had been able to find so many. There was a neat little pile of all the possible cases in one corner near Bishop's desk where he was going through them personally.

Maki walked in, at some point, wearing what looked like someone's oversized sweats with Antoinette tight on her heels. Bishop then also put them to work reading.

It was probably close to eleven at night before Bishop put down the last of the confirmed cases and stood to survey the room. Everyone paused to look at him.

"We've got something, at least," Bishop began. "The earliest cases are in Maine; then he moves south until he hits Boston where he exclusively killed right under our noses for about two months. He continued south to Connecticut and Rhode Island before returning to Boston. However, in the past two weeks we only have two confirmed cases: Maki and Khan's." He nodded to them both. "He moved west to the Albany area and then stopped."

"He's waiting for us," Aaron said softly, echoing Yani's own fears.

"Yes," Bishop agreed. "But why Albany? What's in Albany that he wants us to know about before he resumes killing?"

There were a few murmurs and thoughts thrown about, but a sick, churning feeling in Yani's gut said he had the answer.

"I'm from Albany," Yani said loudly, cutting through the rest of the chatter. "All of my family is in Albany. What if I'm not the only one in my family born with eyes-that-see that he wants to steal? Or maybe he just wants revenge because I helped everyone escape last time?"

"He distracted us by sending us after the leprechaun in New Hampshire while he set up shop in Albany," Aaron agreed, his own voice tight with worry. He had spent a lot of time over the last few years with Yani's family and had been welcomed with open arms. Yani knew Aaron liked them all, and seeing them hurt would devastate them both.

Yani pulled out his phone and dialed his mother's cell. His heart was in his throat as he waited for the call to go through, and every ring that she didn't answer had him shaking.

"Yani? It's so late. Is everything okay?" Mom's voice came through after the third ring, and Yani let out a heavy breath of air.

"Yeah, Mom, everything's okay. I never called to ask if you and Dad got to Chicago safely."

Mom laughed. "Our flight was uneventful. We got in about ten this morning. You should see the baby! He's the cutest little thing!" Yani could hear his Dad's distinctive rumble in the background for a moment. "Your dad says hi," Mom said. "We have to be up early tomorrow for Shabbat services. We'll call on Sunday after the bris to tell you how it went."

"Okay. Is Shira with you?" Yani asked.

"She has school. Lotan took her for the weekend. Talk to you on Sunday, Yani." Mom said her goodbyes and Yani hung up. He waited a few seconds for the call to disconnect before putting in Shira's cell number and hitting Call.

Uncle Lotan was one of Mom's two older brothers. Grandpa Gideon had moved in with Lotan after his wife passed away to keep from having to endure an old folks' home—Grandpa's words, not Yani's—and helped keep track of Uncle Lotan's rambunctious twins. They had been such a handful when they were younger that Uncle Lotan and his wife hadn't wanted to have any more kids. However, they had a big house with lots of empty rooms so had quickly become the babysitters of Yani's cousins. Shira should be fine there, except as three rings became four and then five, Yani's heart stopped beating.

The phone connected, and Yani realized Shira must have left her phone downstairs when she went to bed and it had taken Uncle Lotan this long to figure out what was ringing. But it wasn't Uncle Lotan's voice on the other end of the line.

"How nice of you to call," Cain said in a genial tone. "I have been expecting you for hours and was starting to grow bored. You are lucky I didn't decide to entertain myself. Children are so small, but they squeal so nicely when I break them. There's hardly enough flesh to suffice, but sometimes it's nice to practice more intricate work on smaller bodies."

"What do you want, Cain?" Yani forced out through a throat tight with tears and fury. He was clutching at his phone as if he could magically transport himself to Shira's side and protect her.

"I want your eyes," Cain hissed. "I invested a lot of magic into you, idiot human. I created a construct that fed on humans for three years, then killed it and used its blood to enhance your innate sight. My power runs through your veins, and I have let you run free for long enough. I'm calling you back to my side now, boy. Obey or suffer the consequences."

Yani had no doubt what those consequences would be.

"Where do I meet you?" Yani asked immediately.

He could practically feel Cain's cold smile through the phone. "The house where I took your family will suffice. I have set up a doorway to lead you to me."

"I'm on my way, Cain. Don't hurt my family," Yani insisted.

Cain laughed. "There's not a single, solitary drop of magic in any of their puny bodies. They're useless to me alive or dead. However, they still scream beautifully. If I wait too long for you to come, I may try making a little music."

"I'm coming, Cain," Yani reiterated.

"Yes, from Boston. I'll see you in four hours."

The call ended and Yani pulled the phone away from his ear with a gasp. He looked around the room wildly, finally focusing on Bishop, who had his own phone held to his ear.

"A van is waiting for you out front. The driver has explicit instructions to break every traffic law to get you to Albany in time and permission to use spells to keep the police from noticing. Get whatever you need and go. I'll have backup on your tail as soon as I roust them from their beds."

Yani went, dashing out of the filing room. They weren't far from the front door, and he burst outside a few moments later. A large van was waiting, the engine running, and Yani climbed inside. He was followed by Aaron, Brandon, Luke, Khan, and Maki, who all found seats.

"I'll scout ahead," Antoinette insisted. "What's the address?"

It took Yani a moment of frantic thinking to remember that he had Lotan's address in his phone. He found it and told Antoinette and the driver where to go. The van took off with a screech of tires on pavement before Yani could fumble for his seat belt. Antoinette jumped away, moving far faster than the van, especially since she didn't have to keep to the roads.

The next three and a half hours were the tensest Yani could ever remember in his life. There was Shira's birth, when all the aunts and uncles and grandparents had been hovering worriedly in the waiting room for news about whether Shira had been born alive. There had also been sitting at Gramma's bedside listening to her story about how she had escaped the Nazis while waiting for her to die. This was far worse than all of that combined.

Cain was evil, plain and simple, and Yani couldn't trust him to wait for Yani to get there before starting to hurt his family. It was lucky that none of them had magic, or Yani knew he would be rushing to save their bodies, but there was still no guarantee that wasn't what he was doing right now.

The van rocketed around the turns, swerving around other cars on the road at high speeds. Every once in a while, the driver would mumble something, and they would flash without notice past a cop car waiting in one of the turnarounds on the highway.

"Breathe, Yani," Khan said softly. Another round of the strange magical tingles went through his body. "Focus on what you can feel right now. We're doing everything we can, so you need to stay calm."

What could Yani feel right now? He could feel the ache in his hands from clutching the seat belt strap extremely tightly in his fists. He could hear his gasping breaths full of choked-back tears. Yani peeled his fingers open and used his sleeve to wipe his eyes and face clean. Focus was important right now. Aaron's magic was filling the van as he prepped his spells for battle. A strange, spicy scent was in the air as Brandon and Maki called on their other halves.

Yani looked out the window in time to see the first glimpse of the castle-like mansion that dominated Albany's skyline. They were fifteen minutes away. Maybe closer, given just how fast they were driving. Yani began to recognize the neighborhood within a few minutes of them pulling off the highway. They passed the street that led to his own house and continued a few more blocks to where Lotan lived.

The driver stopped the van a few houses down, and they all piled out onto the sidewalk. Yani would have run to Lotan's house immediately, but Khan clamped his hands down on Yani's shoulders, and Aaron shot him a warning took.

"We go in every doorway holding hands or with linked arms," Aaron insisted. "He's going to transport us to his cave again, and I don't want only Yani to go and then have the door shut behind him. Yani, you never got a look at Cain with your eyes enhanced, so I want to know if you see anything on or around him that might give us an edge. Khan, same with you, since you've never seen him before. Maki and Brandon, I need you to distract Cain. Keep him busy while Khan and I figure out a spell to stop him. Luke, get to the hostages. Pull them to safety in the dream world if you can. If not, get them up and ready to run."

"I'll help with the distraction," Antoinette insisted as she dropped to the sidewalk beside Maki. They shared a brief glance that lingered for a little longer than it would have had they just been friends before Antoinette turned back to Aaron. "The house is quiet. I didn't go inside, but I can't sense anything alive or moving."

Aaron nodded to show he understood. "Any other concerns?" he asked the group. When he didn't get an answer, he took a deep breath and turned to face Lotan's house. "Let's go."

They walked quickly down the sidewalk and up the driveway to the front door, and then everyone linked hands or arms. Aaron's shield spell was shining brilliantly in front of him as he reached out to turn the handle. It was unlocked, and the door opened smoothly, but Yani didn't see Lotan's entrance hall behind it. The space was pitch black, just like the portal Yani barely remembered from last time.

"Let's go," Aaron repeated to steel himself and everyone else. He stepped through the doorway and vanished, pulling everyone in after him one by one. Yani stepped into the blackness resolutely. He had to save his family. The time for tears and fear was over.

Yani emerged on the other side of the portal into a familiar cave. The space was riddled with stalactites and stalagmites towering overhead. There was a large burnt area a few feet in front of him, and with a pang, Yani remembered the ifrit they had defeated there. They strode forward together as a group, and within moments, Yani saw the rest of what he remembered.

The stone altar where he had lain helplessly as Cain painted on him in fresh blood was off to one side. The tripod, thankfully empty, where Rachel had hung so he could collect her blood was nearby. Even the cages where Luke, Brandon, and Aaron had been kept were in the same place. Yani could see Grandpa Gideon, Uncle Lotan, Aunt Talya, the twins, and Shira lying in those cages. They weren't moving, and Yani could only hope that they were only unconscious or asleep.

"I see you brought friends," Cain said, sounding genial again as they strode into view from around a huge stalagmite. Cain was still wearing the long cloak that hid all of their features from sight, but the voice was exactly the same: young and cruel. "More fun for me. I would say surrender yourself, but you and I both know you won't. Besides, it would be far too boring if I didn't have to subdue you under my foot first.

"So, here's how this is going to go. We will all fight. I will defeat you; then I will take your eyes. But before I finish killing you, I will kill all your friends and family where you can hear it perfectly well. Then I will allow you to slowly die."

"Let's get started then," Aaron growled, "and let us prove to you that you are the one that's going to lose!"

Cain laughed. "We'll see."

Cain vanished from sight in a blur that Yani couldn't follow. Everyone scattered. There was a crash of fists hitting flesh, and Yani looked up to see Antoinette pulling back from hitting Cain in the stomach with her fist. She was apparently fast enough to keep up with Cain—but not strong enough. He flung her away a moment later, but he had gotten low enough that Maki could reach him. She dug her claws into his leg, drawing blood and yanking him down to the floor where Brandon leaped forward to gauge long claw marks out of Cain's back.

Even though he was bleeding heavily, Cain was still laughing as if this were just a grand old time to him. Magic flashed and Brandon and Maki were thrown off Cain before they could do too much damage. Aaron spat out a spell of his own, and Brandon and Maki slowed before they could hit the stone floor with damaging force.

"You can't defeat me with your puny abilities," Cain told Aaron, still laughing.

"But I can," Khan insisted.

Stalagmites snapped with earth-shuddering crashes as a gigantic black dragon filled the cavern. Magic flared from Khan, sending Cain flying, but Cain spun effortlessly in the air and landed softly a few feet away.

Their spells weren't working. Yani needed to focus and see if anything his eyes could tell him would help them. However, all he could see of Cain was the billowing cloak. It was black like the portal had been black, which meant it was magic of some sort. It didn't sparkle or shine like the magic Yani usually saw. In fact, he would say it did the exact opposite.

"I think his cloak eats magic," Yani called. "It's absorbing your spells and keeping Cain's true form hidden from us."

"So we remove it," Khan roared. Fire flared from his mouth, and Yani tensed in immediate fear, but as Cain swerved in the air to avoid it, Maki got her claws in his leg again. She went after his cloak with her other paw, digging her claws into the fabric and ripping off large pieces. They fluttered to the ground like regular cloth, but when they hit the ground, they sizzled like water dropped on a hot stove before vanishing in a puff of smoke.

"You dare!" Cain snarled. He had stopped laughing. "Fine, so I won't wait to take the eyes-that-see first! I'll kill you all now and make him suffer all the more for it!"

Yani lost sight of Luke in the madness. Yani couldn't help glancing over at the cages briefly and saw that two of them were open and empty. Shira and the twins had vanished, which hopefully meant Luke had been able to force them into the dream world. Only Uncle Lotan, Aunt Talya, and Grandpa Gideon were left. Yani left Luke to it and refocused on the battle.

The cloak had been shredded all along one side. Yani could see the pale flash of leg and bare foot. The skin wasn't pale like Yani was pale—too much Polish blood in his veins—it was more as if there was an absence of color. Yet, that was wrong too. Cain's skin looked like a crystal or prism, reflecting a rainbow of colors when light hit it.

He wasn't an unseelie sidhe at all. "He's a fairy!" Yani yelled.

Aaron spat something, quickly echoed by Khan. Cain froze in midair and let out an ear-piercing shriek.

Fairies were magical creatures much like witches and mages, but they were more like dragons in that instead of using spells to cast magic, they were magic. They could absorb the magic of others, which explained a lot of Cain's actions over the past few years, and then use it to power their spells.

The cloak fell away from Cain entirely, revealing more rainbow-colored skin and the fact that Cain did, in fact, have a male-shaped body. He was completely naked without the cloak, and his dick was as rainbow as the rest of him. Cain had a pair of large, see-through wings on his back, and they flapped in the air ineffectually as whatever spells Aaron and Khan used held him in place.

"We know how to stop a fairy, no matter how much magic you've stolen," Aaron told Cain sharply. "You're under arrest for over fifty murders that we know about. You will be prosecuted to the full extent of magical law."

Instead of continuing to fight or even surrendering, Cain started laughing again. "You're going to prosecute me? And here I was starting to give you idiots some credit." The rainbow sheen to his skin suddenly vanished, and Cain dropped bonelessly in place like a doll with its strings cut.

"It's another damned simulacrum!" Aaron swore. His magic dropped from the body and he spun around, looking for Cain again.

Yani spun around, too, trying to find Cain with his special eyes amid the gloom of the cave. Except, Cain didn't need to be present to control his simulacrum, so maybe he wasn't there at all; he certainly hadn't been anywhere near the coalition building to pilot Felipe. At least, Yani didn't think so. What if Cain had been nearby? What if he worked for the coalition, and that was how he was able to keep track of their movements so easily. That speculation would have to wait. If it was true, Cain had to be somewhere in the cavern, and they needed to find him fast.

"Yani! Watch out!" Aaron screamed.

Yani turned and his body immediately froze in place. A ball of fire was coming at him, inching slowly closer. It was round, like a hand, and the flames shooting off it like fireworks were similar to fingers. It was the very worst of his nightmares come back to life again, and he couldn't help staring at it helplessly as it flew closer.

Something hit him from the side, sending him sprawling to the floor and out of the path of the flaming missile. The ball of flames hit, and the body shielding Yani convulsed on top of him.

Yani frantically pulled himself out from under the body and crawled around on the floor to slap at the flames burning Khan's shirt.

"Khan! Khan!" Yani yelled. The fire burned his hands, but it wasn't entirely real. He would have blisters from the heat, but nothing was blackened like real fire would do.

"You won't steal my magic like this!" Khan hollered upward. His body was human, but there was something draconian about his face. The area from his nose to his chin was elongated like a snout, and the black scales were thicker than Yani remembered. "I won't allow it!"

Magic was flung from his body in a massive wave that sent Yani sprawling to the ground. He blinked spots out of his eyes and gaped at the destruction. Stalactites were falling from the ceiling with massive crashes of stone and stalagmites were toppling over. The area directly around them was safe within the eye of the storm, but Khan was completely destroying the rest of the cavern in his attempt to find Cain.

Khan was panting for breath, but the magic wave had at least extinguished the flames. Black blood flowed from Khan's middle where the fireball had hit him, sluggishly coating the floor and Yani's knees where he knelt next to Khan.

"Stop fighting," Yani said frantically. "We need to get you to help!"

Khan laughed, but it sounded tired. "It is far too late for that, I am afraid." His eyes flicked pointedly downward toward his feet, and Yani followed his gaze with dawning horror. Khan's body was fading away. Yani could see the stone floor through Khan's feet and his toes had already completely vanished. "I do not have enough magic left to hold on to a physical form."

"You're dying," Yani stated baldly, but it came out more of a croak as his throat closed with yet more tears. He had done enough crying today, yet he couldn't help himself. "We never—" They had never done a lot of things, including have that talk about where their relationship might go.

"I know and I am sorry, Yani. There are things I must tell you before my time runs out. Listen close. First, Aaron loves you with his entire body and soul. He gave me strict instructions on how to treat you right, and I could see his love for you in every word. I know you still love him, too, and if I had not been in the picture, distracting you, you might already be back together. Tell him I am sorry for that."

"You're not a distraction!" Yani insisted. He wiped his eyes to clear away his tears and saw with horror that Khan was transparent up to his knees.

"Hush. I was, but I will not be after this. Go back to him, and this time, if he starts acting odd, smack him a few times and insist on a healing spell. He knows to listen to you now."

Yani nodded wordlessly, and Khan smiled gently at him.

"Do not cry over me," Khan said. He lifted one of his hands to brush away some of the tears on Yani's cheek. "I am not really dying. Once I have gathered enough magic again, I will be able to resume my physical form. Unfortunately, it will be long past your lifetime before I will be capable of that feat. I will watch over you as best as I am able, so look to the sky and smile for me every once in a while."

"I will," Yani said, giving Khan a tremulous smile now just to show he could.

"I have one last thing to tell you," Khan added. He was see-through up to his waist now, and breathing heavily, despite how quickly he was speaking. "Cain is an utter idiot, and the fact that he doesn't think so is his greatest weakness. Remember that. If he had been intelligent, he would not have simply tried to enhance your eyesight. Those with eyes-that-see also have the propensity to have other senses as advanced. Ears-that-hear, mouth-that-tastes, skin-that-feels, and nose-that-smells. I have been trying to slowly open your senses to allow you access to them, something that Cain should have known to do if he was going to steal all of your power."

"The tingling magical feeling I've been getting over the last few days?" Yani asked.

"I thought you had sensed what I was doing. There is no longer time for me to do it delicately. You will need all of your senses to be able to defeat Cain once and for all, and I am going to give them to you now. Please forgive me for the pain I am about to cause you."

"I forgive you?" Yani said, wondering what Khan was talking about.

The strange tingling feeling ran through his body again, except this time it didn't stop. It grew and grew until Yani felt like his entire body was vibrating. Then, it stopped.

Yani could hear everything. Khan's magic wave still wreaking havoc on the cave resonated against a different sort of magic—Aaron's magic—that sang brightly. Underneath it all was the low undertone of evil. He could smell it too, and feel it impacting against his skin, and taste it in his mouth—acrid versus sweet. It was so much, too much, and Yani could feel himself screaming even if he could no longer hear himself over the cacophony of magic.

He clapped his hands over his ears, shut his mouth tight, and tried not to breathe, but it wasn't nearly enough. It all hurt and he was quickly screaming again.

Yani's eyes were still fine, though, and the last thing he saw before he had to close them to block out something, anything, was Khan's smile before his body vanished completely.

"Yani!" Yani could faintly hear Aaron's voice, and then Aaron's hands touched him, and there was so much magic that it was going to shake Yani's entire body apart. Blackness came a moment later, blissfully pulling Yani away.

*

Cain was seething. He was a fool, played by his own game. He couldn't even defeat one measly dragon. The creature had utterly destroyed Cain's home—he would have to locate another suitable one now—and the dragon's magic had overpowered Cain's own for one critical moment. He was injured, bleeding lightly from a scratch he had endured by being flung into a sharp bit of stone when the dragon's death spell had hit.

Not only hadn't he been able to withstand the dragon, but the mage had also grown in strength. The mage had withstood the dragon's power. Bright, horrible wings of power had erupted from him, encircling the rest of their merry band of idiots to protect them from the dragon's onslaught. Only Cain had been injured in the attack.

He ought to go down there and end them all now. The one with eyes-that-see was writhing on the ground, his mind unconscious while his body continued to be in great pain. At his side was the mage, chanting healing spells and wasting his magic. The two were-creatures and the vampire would be no trouble to defeat. Neither would the incubus that had somehow managed to punch through his magical shields and secrete his prisoners safely away from his influence.

Cain should go kill them all now with one swoop of magic. Yet, what if he failed?

His best construct, his favorite, had been utterly destroyed in the fight. The fairy had long been dead and the body Cain's favorite to inhabit for a time, but it was gone now and with its loss, Cain had also lost his anonymity. He would have to confront them with his real body and risk himself.

He was the most powerful being in the world, Cain reminded himself sternly. A little stumble was nothing to be ashamed about. It was just a lapse in concentration, easily overcome, and look how weak his enemy was. He had captured them once and had lured them to him a second time. He could do it again whenever.

No, he would have to wait until he had another body to inhabit. That was being smarter, overcoming his little misstep in his quest to take down the coalition and rule the magical world in its stead.

It meant letting his prey go again, but in truth, they had been dealt a heavier blow than he. The dragon was gone, and it would be a while before the eyes-that-see was functional again, given how much pain it looked like he was in. Cain, therefore, had time to get himself ready for one final battle.

Cain watched as they all gathered around the incubus, who punched through Cain's shields yet again. Although, the shields were probably terribly weakened thanks to the dragon's final bit of magic. It was just an incubus, and sex wasn't real power. They vanished, leaving Cain alone in his disintegrating cave once more.

Soon he would kill them all. Very soon. First, though, he had to rebuild a bit of his power. Then he would destroy the entire coalition...down to every last brick.

*

Maki woke at dusk when she felt Antoinette stir next to her. Antoinette looked over guiltily at Maki, sorry for waking her when they both still needed sleep. It had been a tough few days for them.

Fighting Cain had been unlike anything Antoinette had experienced before. She never wanted to do it again, yet at the same time, she wanted to continue the fight to keep everyone safe from evil. It was honorable and wonderful.

Antoinette had never before been a fighter. She had been a slave, owned and abused by various masters throughout her life. Until she had met Maki. Now Antoinette had the drive to fight in order to keep Maki safe. If that meant fighting Cain again, or anyone else for that matter, she would do it. With Maki at her side, she would enjoy it too.

"This necklace," Maki said softly to Antoinette. She was holding the sakura charm in one palm and speaking shyly to it. "It has powerful protection magic and a very specific tradition to it. A mother would always give it to her oldest son, who would gift it in turn to his beloved bride, who would then pass it on to her oldest son in an endless cycle. Until it reached my mother. Okasan was only able to have me, and she instructed me to pass it on to my son. But tradition dictates that I should first give it to my beloved, who will pass it on to our son."

She held the necklace out toward Antoinette and looked up at Antoinette for the first time since she had started speaking. There was hope and desire in her eyes, and then a touch of wonder when Antoinette wordlessly reached out to take the charm from Maki's hand.

Antoinette didn't know what to say. It was everything she had ever wanted to hear from Maki.

"You're certain?" Antoinette couldn't help asking, as if the confirmation would change the light, happy feeling buoying her heart.

"Very," Maki answered simply.

"Then help me put it on," Antoinette finally said, letting the charm dangle by the chain.

Maki leaned forward to undo the clasp and slip the necklace around Antoinette's throat. The charm dangled just above her breasts, shining against her dark skin. Maki was so close and her body so warm. Antoinette turned her head just a bit more until she could feel Maki's breath against her lips. It was so easy to press forward until their lips touched, and with a happy groan, Maki deepened their kiss.

Much later, after a well-deserved nap, Maki rolled over to face Antoinette. Her face was serious.

"I'm going to continue aging," she said softly, "while you will remain as you are now."

"You want to be a vampire," Antoinette finished for Maki, gently reaching out to touch the healing puncture marks on Maki's neck. Maki nodded. "There is a procedure we must follow first, set out by the vampire council. You have to remain human and interested for five years. If you still want to become a vampire after those five years are up, then I am allowed to change you. We will have to wait, but, Maki, I want you to think about the consequences. Weres that are turned into vampires have different reactions. Some of them lose their were form entirely, while others become more bestial. There's no telling how it will affect you."

"But it will allow me to remain by your side for eternity," Maki insisted. "So we'll wait five years and see what happens between then."

It was Antoinette's turn to nod mutely, but she couldn't stop the smile from growing on her face. "It could be a long five years. What do you want to do until then?" She ruffled the sheets covering their nakedness pointedly.

Maki laughed happily and smiled. "Plenty of that, of course, but do you think we can continue helping Brandon out? His friends all seem like such nice people. It would be so nice to have friends."

"I was thinking the same thing," Antoinette admitted. "We should go speak with Bishop Karr and see how Yani's doing. I heard they were able to calm him down yesterday, but he's still unconscious."

"Shower first?" Maki asked with a grin that said they should do much more than just shower. Antoinette answered that grin with her own and hopped off the bed to hurry into the bathroom ahead of a happily giggling Maki.

Epilogue

"I would have a word with you, Bishop," Martin said sharply. He stood politely outside the open office door to wait for an invitation to enter. Yakov hovered worriedly at Martin's side, awaiting the bad news they both knew was imminent.

"Martin!" Bishop gasped in surprise, jumping to his feet and hurrying around his overloaded desk to greet them. "You should have called to say you were coming!" There were dark circles under Bishop's eyes that Martin did not remember from his last visit, and the wrinkles from exhaustion were more pronounced on Bishop's face.

"We did call," Martin said in explanation. "We called Yani dozens of times and left numerous messages, but never received any response. When we called your office here, your secretary informed us that you were out of the office for the foreseeable future. We could only assume something terrible had occurred, and Yakov insisted we be on the next flight out."

"Take a seat, please," Bishop said with a wave toward the two guest chairs on the closer side of his desk. "You are right that something has happened. Let me fill you in." He must have caught sight of Yakov's pained frown because he held up his hands in placation. "Yani is still alive and is slowly healing. Don't worry. Let me tell you the full story, and then I'll take you to see him."

They sat, and Bishop hurried to retake his own seat. He took a deep breath to stall, as if he wasn't entirely certain when to start the story, before speaking.

"It actually started about nine months ago. Aaron started acting odd, but we ignored it, thinking he was simply embroiled in his studies. Only, his behavior continued to grow worse until Yani was forced to break up with Aaron to escape what had apparently become a loveless partnership. It was the wakeup call Aaron needed, as he went to get help. He returned just in time to save Yani, who was starting to act odd himself. I am sad to say that I missed all of this, too busy with coalition work to keep the eye on them that I meant to. For two years they handled every problem without needing my help, and I got complacent at the very moment I shouldn't have."

Bishop sounded truly contrite, as if all the problems were his fault alone. Martin knew that couldn't possibly be true, but he also could tell that Bishop wasn't prepared to believe Martin if Martin said anything to dissuade him.

"Were you able to figure out what was attacking them?" Yakov asked. He sounded worried, but then, he had been the one to insist they travel all the way here to see whether Yani needed their help.

"A form of voodoo from Africa," Bishop replied immediately. "It attacked their psyches, trapping Aaron in his studies and Yani in a fugue of depression. I believe it also blocked your calls, as you might have been able to pull Yani out of the spell's influence had he spoken with you. It would explain why he missed your calls."

"Was it Cain?" Martin asked, wondering who had enspelled them.

"It was." Bishop didn't sound the least bit doubtful. "Cain had used a spell to force Brandon, my grandson, as well as a werepanda named Maki into their animal forms. Unable to change back, they were both starting to go a bit mad, I believe. Aaron went to his mother for tutoring with their curse, was also healed of his own malady, and brought that healing back to his friends. With everyone back in fighting form, Yani quickly discovered a trail of bodies Cain had left, leading us directly to Albany."

"My family!" Yakov gasped.

"Exactly. We were able to fight off Cain in the end, but not without heavy losses. One of our allies, a dragon Yani was a close friend with, passed away in the fight. Something also happened to Yani's magic, which is all we have been able to glean so far, and he hasn't been able to wake up since. Our best healer believes he will wake eventually, and that the sleep is a way of protecting himself and healing. I will have a room prepared for you to stay in, so you can wait until Yani wakes if you would like."

Martin glanced over at Yakov and saw the familiar stubborn tilt to his jaw. Yakov wouldn't be going anywhere until he saw for himself that his family was safe.

"We appreciate the generosity," Martin said.

Bishop stood, so they stood as well. "Let me show you to Yani's side," he said.

"Oh!" a woman's voice gasped from the open doorway. Martin turned to look and saw Antoinette, the vampire woman he had left in charge, standing there with a small Asian woman at her side. "Master Martin!"

"Antoinette, Martin is here to see Yani," Bishop explained. Martin assumed Bishop was giving her warning not to worry about him coming to take over her territory, but she wasn't worried about that any longer. He could have it if he wanted—he read that in her eyes—but he also saw a spark of true inner strength there as well. She was no longer bravado covering fear, but quickly becoming a real leader. It was just as he had hoped for her.

"Of course," Antoinette said with a polite nod to Martin. The woman at her side gave him a proper Japanese bow. "If Maki and I might speak with you, Alpha Karr, after your business with Martin is concluded? We would like to speak with you about joining Brandon and Yani in working to protect our people from harm."

Bishop's face immediately brightened, some of the age and exhaustion falling away as he smiled at them.

"Would you prefer to join Brandon and Yani as part of their group, or would you like to start a group of your own? I would love to have two investigative teams on staff. For large assignments, like going after Cain, I would expect both groups to work as one under Aaron's leadership. Think on it and let me know."

Antoinette shared a look with Maki, and suddenly Martin knew where Antoinette had found the spark of strength she was nurturing into true power. Love was always a great motivator.

"The latter," Antoinette answered for them both. "We don't need to think on it. Maki and I would like our own team, led by Aaron."

"I will see it done," Bishop replied. "I'll set up interviews for the rest of your team starting next week and see about what Aaron wants to do to train you all. Also,

Antoinette, if you would take the time to go through the wards on the vampire house, I would appreciate it. Removing the entry permissions for every vampire and creature that hasn't lived there in the last six months would prevent another incident like the one with Felipe."

"I'll do that," Antoinette agreed. "Thank you, Alpha Karr." Antoinette nodded politely to the room, and Maki bowed before they turned and hurried off together.

"When Aaron's human lifespan has ended, you will still have Antoinette to lead your teams of investigators," Martin said, wondering whether Bishop knew that too.

"Yes, and hopefully in another forty years, Antoinette will finally learn to lead. You put a slave in charge of the vampires, Martin," Bishop said pointedly. "You weakened us because of it."

"Did I?" Martin asked sharply. "For the short term of two years, maybe, but give her a hundred years, and I do believe Antoinette will become one of the most powerful coven leaders in the world. She just needed the opportunity, and between your and my influence, she is slowly starting to get there. Two years is a small price to pay for what she will bring to your coalition in the end."

"That's true enough," Bishop agreed easily. "Well, let me show you to Yani before something else walks through my office door to distract us."

Bishop led the way through the many hallways of the coalition building until they reached the residence portion. Yani had been given a private room, and Bishop knocked briefly before letting himself in.

Aaron was sitting in a chair pulled up to Yani's bedside. He looked gray and even more exhausted than

Bishop, if that were possible, and his fingers were pressed to a shimmering globe that encircled the bed and Yani. Aaron said something that Martin didn't understand, which was remarkable; throughout the years, Martin had made a point of learning at least a modicum of every language he encountered, including quite a few that were considered dead now. Although, he was quite fluent in Yiddish now, thanks to Yakov, and he thought he might have recognized a word or two of Aaron's spell.

The globe flared briefly before returning to a low glow, and Aaron stood to greet them.

"No change since you were last here," he told Bishop.

"What happened?" Yakov asked worriedly. He strode past them to the globe where he could look inside and see Yani sleeping on the bed.

"We're not entirely sure," Aaron said with a sigh and a quick glance over his shoulder at Yani that told Martin just how worried Aaron was.

Their relationship had hit a rough patch, given Yani's various phone messages over the last few months, but that was part of the course of life. What made relationships strong was the ability for partners to work together to overcome the rough spots and to forge an even stronger bond in the end. Aaron was willing to try, which meant the onus fell on Yani to decide whether he was willing to take Aaron back. There was always a chance their relationship would come to an end instead, and Aaron would need to learn to accept that, but Martin had a feeling they were going to be okay.

"Yani and Khan were separated from us by an attack. Khan was gravely injured, but I thought Yani was okay.

Then a massive spell wave erupted from Khan. I had to protect everyone else, and by the time the spell wave faded, and I could drop my shield, Yani was screaming in pain. The doctor says his senses went into overdrive. He was clutching at his ears as if they hurt, and any time I touched his skin with magic, he screamed, even while unconscious."

Martin looked between Aaron and Yani thoughtfully for a few moments before an idea dawned on him. "Have you ever heard of ears-that-hear?" Martin asked and then waited for Aaron's eyes to widen in realization. He spun to look at Yani, although what his eyes saw, given all the spell work he had been doing on Yani, was probably completely different to what Martin could see. "It is not common for those touched by vampires to have more than one enlightened sense, but it is not unheard of."

"What if Khan opened all of Yani's senses before he died? The sudden influx of sensation would drive anyone mad!" Aaron spun to look at Bishop. "Get Gem'ma. We need to reformulate the healing spells." He spun back to Yani, quickly putting his hands upon the globe. He started speaking again, and Martin heard ancient Hebrew, the precursor to modern Hebrew and Arabic and a language he thought was long dead, fall from Aaron's lips. Someone had been studying in the last two years if he could manage spell work in that language so smoothly. Martin had no doubt Yani was in good hands. It was a relief to see.

"Let us get out of your way," Martin said firmly. "We'll visit again later." He led Yakov from the room. They needed to feed after their long journey, so they headed outside, but Yakov hesitated by the door.

"Yani is mending," he said softly.

"Yes," Martin agreed, "but he could use a friendly face when he wakes. We will stay for a while to help him continue to heal. He should wake soon."

Yakov smiled, and Martin couldn't help smiling back, pleased to see Yakov happy again. They jumped into the night to go find food.

*

Everything was muffled. It was like earmuffs covered his entire body, and Yani didn't like the feeling. He opened his eyes and then blinked a few times, trying to get them to focus. It didn't work. Everything had a soft, blurred edge to it. Yani carefully turned his head to see if the rest of the room looked the same and heard someone gasp in surprise.

"Yani! You're awake!" Aaron said, except his voice also sounded strangely muffled.

"What's wrong with me?" Yani asked, reaching up to rub his eyes to see if that would help. "I can't see properly, or hear?"

"You don't remember what happened?" Aaron asked gently.

Yani did remember. Khan pushing him out of the way of Cain's spell and then fading away to nothingness. Yani's throat tightened with tears, but like the rest of his body, his emotions were slightly muted and the expected tears didn't fall.

Before Khan died, he had said a few things to Yani. The first, that Aaron still loved Yani, was plainly evident in what little Yani could see and hear of Aaron. The worry and exhaustion from sitting at Yani's bedside for however long Yani had been unconscious this time was clear in the waver of Aaron's voice and the way he had immediately jumped to Yani's side.

The second thing Khan had said Yani thought might explain the muffled feeling.

"I have had eyes-that-see my entire life, Aaron. Khan's spell didn't affect them, so you can drop whatever protective spell you've put up," Yani explained.

"Of course!" Aaron gasped.

Yani could see his hands press up against something and heard him recite a spell, and slowly everything around him came into proper focus. A circle of power surrounded Yani: a shining, glittering globe that was so strong Yani thought he might be able to see it without his special eyes. Aaron looked as tired as he had sounded, with dark circles under his eyes, but the small smile that lifted his lips briefly said how relieved he was that Yani was awake.

"What about the rest of your senses?" Aaron asked. "Is anything off about them? We created a dampening spell to help, and the plan is to slowly wean you off of it until you have control again."

"I think the spell is too strong?" Yani asked. "Everything feels muffled. I'm not hearing you correctly. I also remembered Khan's death, and I didn't cry like I should have."

Aaron nodded and focused on the globe again with another spell. "I don't want to bring it up too much and have you relapse. Tell me when things feel normal again."

Yani waited, listening to Aaron say the spells, and slowly he began to feel normal. He could hear Aaron's voice perfectly fine, and there was an ache in his chest that said he was feeling emotions again. The tears that had been threatening began to fall.

"Enough," Yani gasped.

"Sorry! I took it too far. I'll lower it some," Aaron said frantically.

"No, it's fine. I'm just..." Yani paused to gulp for breath and angrily wiped the tears from his face with one sleeve. "Khan isn't really dead. I know that. But he lost his physical form saving my life."

"I'm so sorry, Yani," Aaron whispered. He dabbed at his own eyes. "I know you liked him. I liked him too."

"I did like him, but I never got the chance to find out if I loved him," Yani admitted. "I wanted to have that chance, so I'm crying just as much because he's gone as for what could have been." Aaron nodded but didn't say anything. "But Khan told me that you loved me, and, Aaron, I never stopped loving you. That was part of the reason I had to leave you. I loved you too much, and it was hurting me. But you're back now."

"I'm back now, and I'm prepared to stay," Aaron said firmly. "Whatever that might mean for us."

Yani held out one hand, but was stopped by the globe. Aaron pressed his own hand against the globe over Yani's.

"Let's start over," Yani said after a moment of staring at their hands. "Go on a few dates, see if the spark is still there."

Aaron nodded wordlessly, and Yani noticed tears in his eyes.

But there was something else just as pressing. "Tell me what I've missed. How long was I unconscious? What happened to Shira and Uncle Lotan?"

"Luke got Shira and the rest of your family safe into the dream world while we were distracting Cain. He made them think that the entire night was a strange nightmare, easily forgotten by morning. Bishop has people monitoring them for the time being to make certain Cain stays away."

Yani let out a breath of relief at that. "Any word on Cain? What happened after Khan zapped me?"

Aaron shook his head, visibly disappointed with himself. "I used up too much magic keeping everyone safe from Khan's blast. With three of us down, we needed to get out and regroup. We took down Cain's fairy simulacrum, and Khan destroyed the cave Cain was using, which I'm certain was a big blow. Cain's got to be scrambling to set up a new headquarters and reform his protections, but with the magical community on alert, we've so far been able to contain him."

"So you know where he is?" Yani asked incredulously. "Why hasn't someone taken him down yet?"

"Cain's too strong for any one of us to take on alone, even with the damage we've dealt him. Bishop needs a team that can work together, and we're still all he's got. He's called in a ton of favors from the other coalitions, and we do have individual fighters formed into a loose unit he's using to hound Cain. Until you're healed and our unit is ready to go, that's really all Bishop can do without suffering heavy losses."

"Do we know who Cain is yet?" Yani had to ask. "He seemed to know our exact movements. He was able to send us north so he could work in Albany, and he knew exactly where and when to take Shira."

"Bishop is way ahead of you, actually," Aaron said quickly, before Yani could continue his rushed explanation. "He thinks it might be someone in the administrative offices. They would have had access to all of our files and to us in the dining hall and library. Plus, they could have given Julio the idea to stop staffing the filing room to keep his activities quiet. Bishop is wondering whether the embezzled money might have been funneled to pay for Cain's activities."

"And when Cain heard I was being sent to that office, he arranged for me to get the filing, knowing that thanks to my job, I was trained to notice the strange murders he had been committing," Yani added.

Aaron finished Yani's thought. "That's when he knew it was time to start luring us back to his cave. He just underestimated Maki and Khan."

"But he won't again. We'll have to be even stronger than before," Yani insisted. He paused, looking down at his lap and then back up at Aaron. "That's why Khan forced all my senses open. He said I would need them all to defeat Cain, and he no longer had the time to do it slowly."

"You might be our greatest weapon, then," Aaron said solemnly. "Bishop is planning to hold a memorial ceremony for him in about a week. We'll make sure you're well enough to attend."

"That depends," a new voice said gruffly from the doorway. "If you keep changing the healing spells around him, without the permission of his doctor, neither of you will be well enough to attend."

Yani sat up to look around Aaron and saw Gem'ma standing in the doorway with his arms angrily crossed over his chest. Gem'ma was an extremely short man, about three or four feet, with a brown-colored beard so thick and wild that Yani couldn't tell it apart from his equally thick and wild hair.

"His eyes weren't changed by Khan's meddling, and he couldn't see properly, so I removed that damper. He was also hearing things muffled, so I decreased the intensity of the dampening spells for the rest of his senses."

Gem'ma harrumphed, and his scowl didn't abate in the least. He stuck both hands against the globe and started muttering unhappily under his breath.

"You are extremely lucky that there was no harm done," he snapped angrily at Aaron. "Don't touch the spells again. I'll be back first thing tomorrow morning to check on him, and I'll make whatever changes are needed."

"Yes, sir," Aaron said, although his quickly hidden smile said he didn't care in the least what Gem'ma was demanding.

"Thank you, Gem'ma," Yani said as sincerely as he could.

Gem'ma grunted. "You always bring me an extremely difficult and very interesting case. It keeps life exciting, but try not to get this injured again. I was tapped out for two days after getting these spells set up. I had to remove an imbedded splinter with a pair of tweezers. Can you imagine?" Gem'ma grunted unhappily again before turning and leaving the room as abruptly as he had appeared.

They sat in silence for a few long moments, Yani trying and failing to think of something to say.

"Let me go tell everyone you're awake and see about getting us some dinner," Aaron finally said. He smiled at Yani briefly before levering himself out of the chair and leaving the room.

Yani was only alone for a few minutes before Luke and Brandon came rushing in. They babbled for a bit, asking about how Yani was feeling, before Luke gasped.

"Oh, yeah. I forgot. I took over answering your cell phone while you were unconscious. Your mom called to tell you she got back to Albany in one piece. I told her you had come down with a summer cold, and Aaron was nursing you back to health. After she interrogated me thoroughly, she agreed that Aaron could keep being your nurse, and you were to call her as soon as you felt better."

"Interrogated you?" Yani wasn't certain whether he should be worried or laughing. No one piled on the worry and guilt like a Jewish mother, and Yani's mother was no exception.

"Eh. She thought you had just broken up, but I explained it was just a hiccup and you were both working it out." Luke shrugged. "The guy's barely left your side the entire time you've been unconscious. I figured you'd at least give him a chance."

Yani was silent for a few moments, dragging out Luke's suspense. He was also parsing through what Luke had said and what Yani and Aaron had just spoken about. Calling Khan a hiccup wasn't right; Yani never wanted to hear his relationship with Khan called that again. Yet, at the same time, that was really all his breakup with Aaron was. A magical hiccup. The gris-gris that had thrown Aaron for a loop wasn't Aaron's fault, and if Yani had thought to bring his concerns about Aaron to another mage or to Gem'ma instead of trying to talk Aaron around on his own, they might have discovered that Aaron was cursed that much sooner.

Their breakup was as much Yani's fault as Aaron's. He couldn't penalize Aaron for his own mistakes. Luckily, he had already told Aaron that they would start by going on a few dates to make sure the spark was still there. Their relationship wasn't magically going to be exactly the same as before. There were bruised hearts on both sides, and Khan had changed their dynamic slightly. However, that didn't mean they couldn't make it work again.

"Aaron and I aren't dating again..." He paused to draw out Luke's gasp of dismay. "But we are going to go on a date and see if it takes us in the same direction. If we both still want to be together, I'll move back into the apartment."

Luke squealed happily, grabbing at Brandon to dance around the room. Yani couldn't help smiling with them, wishing he could leave his globe to dance with them. It was amazing to know things might be returning to normal.

"I'm glad to see it's so lively in here," Uncle Yakov said from the doorway.

"Uncle Yakov!" Yani gasped. "What are you doing here?"

Uncle Martin followed him into the room. "We called dozens of times and left no few messages," he explained, "but when you didn't respond, Yakov and I decided to come visit and see if everything is okay. As you can guess, we have been conscripted into the fight with Cain."

Since Uncle Martin was one of the strongest people Yani had ever met, that wasn't surprising.

"Are you strong enough to defeat Cain?" Yani had to ask. Uncle Martin was an extremely old and very powerful vampire.

He laughed. "Ordinarily, I would say yes. There is little in the world that can harm someone who has lived as long as I; however, a dragon is one that could cause me some difficulty. If your dragon was unable to withstand Cain, I believe I would have difficulty as well. I will wait with Bishop for you to heal so we might all work together as a team against Cain."

"So you must heal quickly, Yani," Uncle Yakov added, with Luke and Brandon nodding emphatically behind him. "This battle won't wait for too much longer."

"I'll do my best," Yani agreed.

Everyone pulled up chairs to the bed and started chatting. Aaron returned with Maki and Antoinette in tow, all three of them carrying heavy trays full of food and drink. They laughed and hung out until late that night, and Yani fell asleep knowing his friends and family were still there for him through it all.

*

The memorial occurred two weeks later. Yani was finally out of his protective bubble, but he had to wear a special headband that covered his ears and helped continue dampening his other senses. It was a neat bit of spell work on Aaron's part, grudgingly acknowledged by Gem'ma, who had gotten Aaron's permission to write the spell down and share it among the healing community.

The ceremony was being held on the front driveway. Yani stepped outside behind Aaron and couldn't help stopping to gape incredulously at the great stone dragon that someone had built just beyond the parking area. It looked like Khan, with thick scales and wide wings. Benches had been set up nearby in the parking lot, and once Yani got over his surprise, he started walking toward them.

Luke, Brandon, and Maki were there as well. The sun was shining overhead, so Antoinette, Uncle Yakov, and Uncle Martin couldn't join them, but Yani knew they were present in spirit. Yani also saw other people he recognized, including Arnold, the leader of the werebears.

"He came personally to bring me my things," Maki explained with a gentle smile when she saw what had caught Yani's attention. "Brought an entire moving van down with my furniture and everything. Antoinette and I are going to move it all into the vampire house tonight." Yani couldn't help smiling at her, happy because she was clearly also very happy.

The proceedings started a few minutes later. Yani found a spot on a bench with his friends and watched as candles were lit in Khan's memory and carefully placed around the base of the statue. People who knew Khan stood up to speak, including Bishop and Arnold. It took Yani a while to gather the courage to stand, but he knew he owed Khan at least a few words.

"I only knew Khan a few days, but he quickly became my friend. He helped me through a tough time in my life, and even as his body was fading away, he still took the time to point me in the right direction," Yani said strongly. His heart was aching, but it was a good ache that said he was beginning to heal. "It is my tradition to chant the Mourners Kaddish when we want to remember someone who has left us. Anyone who knows it, feel free to join. Yitgadal v'yit kadash sh'may raba," he chanted, and was happy when Aaron stood to recite it with Yani. (Magnified and sanctified be G-d's great name.) "O'seh shalom beem-romav, hoo ya'ah-seh shalom aleynu v'al kol Yisrael." (Let He who makes peace in the heavens, grant peace to all of us and to all Israel.) "Thank you, Khan," Yani finished softly.

The ceremony ended soon after, and people stood to mingle. Some stopped by the giant snout of the stone dragon to say something private to Khan. Yani ran his fingers down the snout when he had a moment alone, but he had already said his goodbyes. His cheeks were dry.

"Yani, Aaron," Bishop said as he hurried up to them both after Yani had stepped away from the stone dragon. "If I could have a word?" They followed Bishop to an empty corner of the parking lot. "I sent some people I trust to collect Khan's hoard so the coalition could keep it safe until Khan's return. Khan already took care of it, as the hoard had completely vanished. However, we did find this." He pulled a small velvet box out of his pocket and held it out to Yani.

Yani took the box and opened it. Two rings were nestled inside, and Yani picked one up with shaking fingers. It was a silver or white gold braided band with a dragon circled around the band in black onyx stones. The other band was an equally beautiful exact match. The ring buzzed faintly against Yani's skin and had a slight sparkle to it that said it was enchanted.

"Khan left this?" Yani asked, and the tears he had thought he had finished shedding began to fill his eyes again.

"I think he left them for you to share with whomever you choose to spend your life with," Bishop explained softly with a curious glance at Aaron.

Aaron's magic swelled for a brief moment, exploring the ring in Yani's hand and the one still in the box. Yani could see it move through the air like he always could, but he also felt it like an approaching wave in the ocean against his skin. "It has powerful protection magic on it," Aaron said as his magic dissipated.

Yani carefully put the ring back in the box and closed the lid. His free hand drifted to his side and met with Aaron's already reaching out for him. Their hands clasped and held tight. Those rings might have been meant for Yani and Khan to wear, or they might have always been meant for Yani to choose whomever he wanted, but Khan had made his opinion on the matter clear: he thought Yani should be with Aaron. Yani couldn't disagree. They would find a way to work it out.

Yani smiled at Bishop to thank him for the rings and then squeezed Aaron's hand in his. Aaron squeezed back, and they shared a grin that warmed things inside Yani that hadn't been warmed since before the gris-gris.

There was still so much to do to defeat Cain, but at least they had each other again.

About Mell Eight

When Mell Eight was in high school, she discovered dragons. Beautiful, wondrous creatures that took her on epic adventures both to faraway lands and on journeys of the heart. Mell wanted to create dragons of her own, so she put pen to paper. Mell Eight is now known for her own soaring dragons, as well as for other wonderful characters dancing across the pages of her books. While she mostly writes paranormal or fantasy stories, she has been seen exploring the real world once or twice.

Facebook
www.facebook.com/MellEightFiction

Twitter
@MellEight

Website
www.melleightfiction.weebly.com

Other NineStar books by this author

Ge-Mi, Part One

Ge-Mi, Part Two

Supernatural Consultant Series

Dragon Consultant

Also from NineStar Press

Ge-Mi: Part One by Mell Eight

A hundred years ago, evil scientists spliced human genes with those of animals, creating a genetic mutation passed on through the generations. Hated because of their differences, these Ge-Mis live on the fringes of society where they scrounge and scrape to get by.

Nevada is half Ge-Mi and hides that fact behind baggy clothes and by keeping distance between himself and everyone around him. One day, his peaceful life is shattered by an explosion and the arrival of a pack of wolves to sniff out the culprit.

Wolves have excellent noses and as Alpha, Taylor can sniff out every one of Nevada's secrets—and the harder Nevada tries to resist, the more difficult staying away from Taylor becomes.

Wounded Alpha by Mell Eight

While Ryker's body came back from Afghanistan just fine, his mind didn't, and his thoughts wander back there in painful flashbacks that have present-time consequences. In order to avoid hurting anyone, Ryker secludes himself in a cabin in the middle of nowhere. Then Officer Chess Medcull shows up with a case of were-animals being tortured and killed in a way similar to how Ryker almost died in the war. In order to stop the murders, Ryker must face the demons in his head, and maybe, just maybe, allow Chess to help. That is, as long as neither is the next victim.

Kelpie Blue by Mell Eight

When a beautiful blue horse asks Rin to go for a swim, Rin doesn't realize how much his life is about to change. Blue is unlike anyone else Rin has ever met, and the magic of the fae, and of this particular kelpie, is wondrous, but deadly. Rin learns too late he might be in for a swim he won't survive.

Connect with NineStar Press

www.ninestarpress.com

www.facebook.com/ninestarpress

www.facebook.com/groups/NineStarNiche

www.twitter.com/ninestarpress

www.instagram.com/ninestarpress

www.ingramcontent.com/pod-product-compliance
Lightning Source LLC
Chambersburg PA
CBHW020632110726
47899CB00002B/744